TROUBLE

Amy was in train[...] Gymnastic competition[...] as the first reserve. [...] the team, but she'd twi[...]n't help hoping that it would s[...]would have a chance of glory. Then [...]ened that turned all her plans upside down.

It seemed o[...]nutes after Grandma's call that Amy was sitting on the stairs waiting for Richard to get back from the station. Mum had packed a suitcase like a whirl-wind, Richard had bundled baby Helen into her travelling clothes, and the three of them had driven off, leaving Amy to realize that she had to spend at least a weekend with a stepfather she'd never got further than being polite to. She didn't even know what to call him – but now, with Grandad in hospital and on the danger list after an emergency oper-ation, the two of them were going to have to make contact.

In the following days Amy found herself being let in for all sorts of new experiences, for Richard was a lorry driver and didn't want to lose a week's work. She found out what it was like inside his enormous Bedford TK, encountered the world of motorways and transport cafés, and people who spoke quite differently from the ones in Gravesend. It was a messy, unpredictable sort of life, and, to the anxiety of Amy, full of possible disasters. Was it worth it for the sake of seeing a mill with her name on it? Well, she'd have to wait and see.

Jan Mark has a special gift for bringing people – and places – to life, and nervous, sparky Amy is a character many readers from ten upwards will warm to, sometimes be irritated by, and believe in totally.

Jan Mark is one of the most highly acclaimed writers for young people today, and has twice won the Carnegie Medal – for *Thunder and Lightnings* and *Handles*. She was born in London and grew up in Kent. After studying at Canterbury College of Art she taught art in Gravesend. She now lives in Oxford.

Jan Mark

Trouble Half-way

Illustrated by David Parkins

PUFFIN BOOKS

PUFFIN BOOKS

Published by the Penguin Group
27 Wrights Lane, London w8 5TZ, England
Viking Penguin Inc., 40 West 23rd Street, New York, New York 10010, USA
Penguin Books Australia Ltd, Ringwood, Victoria, Australia
Penguin Books Canada Ltd, 2801 John Street, Markham, Ontario, Canada L3R 1B4
Penguin Books (NZ) Ltd, 182–190 Wairau Road, Auckland 10, New Zealand

Penguin Books Ltd, Registered Offices: Harmondsworth, Middlesex, England

First published by Viking Kestrel 1985
Published in Puffin Books 1986
5 7 9 10 8 6 4

Copyright © Jan Mark, 1985
Illustrations copyright © David Perkins, 1985
All rights reserved

Made and printed in Great Britain by
Hazell Watson & Viney Limited
Member of BPCC plc
Aylesbury, Bucks, England
Typeset in Baskerville

For
Neil, Mary and Mike

Chapter One

The road home from school was so steep that when Amy turned the corner by the library she could see the whole estate laid out below like a diagram; Lancaster Drive, Hurricane Crescent, Spitfire Close, Wellington Road, Defiant Avenue and The Runway, where the shops were. The estate was built downhill from an old World War Two airfield and all the streets were named after famous fighting aircraft. It was only later that the council had thought of building on the airfield itself, at the top of the hill, and by that time all the aircraft seemed to have been used up, so the streets were named after flowers. Amy's school was in Harebell Drive but she lived in Hurricane Crescent that grew out of The Runway from the east end and joined it again at the west end, opposite the Co-op.

She could identify her own house, even at this distance, by the washing on the line in the back garden; sixteen white squares, a black half-human shape and a scarlet loop. The white squares were Helen's napkins, the black shape was Amy's leotard and the red loop was her elasticated hairband which she wore for gymnastics. Mrs Varley, over the fence, had only a grey duvet cover on her line, swollen with April wind like a barrage balloon.

As Amy walked down the hill the washing disappeared behind the nearer houses in Wellington Road, and she did not see it again until she had taken the footpath off to the right, beside the Bomber's Moon public house, and was running along the track across the wasteland behind the garages. By this time Mum was in the garden unpegging the napkins, and now that they were out of the way Amy could see something else. Between her house and Mrs Varley's, out on the road at the front, was the blue tractor unit of a lorry. Richard was home.

Amy hopped over the chain link fence beside the garages and took her private short cut to their own gate, into the back garden. Mum did not like her doing that, not because it damaged the fence, which was past repair anyway under the weight of far heavier miscreants than Amy, but because it did not look nice. Mum never complained of Amy waving her legs about when she was wearing the leotard and doing floor exercises on the mat, but it was different, she said, when Amy was wearing her school tunic, or any other skirt. Mum, however, was just going in at the back door with the laundry basket and did not see her approaching.

Richard would not mind if she pole-vaulted over the fence, or over the back gate, either. The gate had dropped a bit on its hinges and he was always saying that he would mend it, but he had been married to Mum for six months

8

now, and the gate was still as it had been when he first moved in. Dad would never have let it get like that.

Helen was on the doorstep, bottom-heavy in napkin and plastic pants like one of those weighted toys that cannot be pushed over. Mum tried to keep her looking nice – in fact Helen showed signs of having been recently refurbished, for her frock was spotless at four o'clock in the afternoon – but Helen pleasantly resisted all attempts at niceness and ended up looking just like all the other two-year-olds on Britton's Field Estate.

'I was out of napkins at thirteen months,' Amy told her, disapprovingly, and stepped over Helen's rolling bulk, into the kitchen. The kitchen looked pristine too, even though it was one of Mum's washdays. Dad had been a carpenter and although he had not been allowed to make structural alterations to a council house he had got everything looking nice; well-made cupboards and doors that did not droop and creak like those of so many other houses on the estate. He had been making improvements to the bathroom when he died, just before Helen was born. Helen thought that Richard was her dad.

Richard, sitting at the table that Dad had made, drinking tea, was the only thing in the kitchen that did not look nice, because he was just home from a five-day trip Up North, sleeping in the back of his lorry and washing in various public conveniences between Gravesend and Preston. When he had had a bath he would blend into the surroundings. He looked up and smiled as she came in.

'Hullo, Amy.'

'Hullo.'

Amy and Richard were still at the stage of being very

9

polite to each other. For a start, Amy never knew what to call him. She would not, like Helen, call him Daddy and she knew that he did not expect her to, but Step-Daddy sounded daft, and she could hardly call him Mr Ermins. Mum did not like her calling him Richard.

'You never called your dad Michael, did you?' Mum had said, unreasonably.

Usually she just made a mumbling noise. It was easier for him: she was Amy to everyone. No one would ever have called her Daughter – not Dad, not Richard.

Mum was folding the napkins into even smaller squares, ready for ironing. 'What d'you want to iron nappies for?' Richard would ask, sometimes. 'Helen won't know any different.'

'Oh, I don't know – it looks . . . nicer,' Mum would say.

'But no one can see them.'

'*I* can see them,' Mum would retort, looking at the tottering pile of flattened napkins on the table, like a stack of sandwiches waiting to be cut into quarters. Richard would be looking at the laundry basket on the floor, full of things still waiting to be ironed.

'Life's too short,' he would say.

Now he was looking at the elastic bandage round Amy's knee.

'How's your leg?'

Mum was looking at her socks, but not saying anything. The socks were gyving round her ankles because she kept tugging at them during lessons and the stretchy part was giving way. Mum ironed socks, too.

'It's not too bad,' Amy said, meaning her knee, and added carefully, because it was Richard who had asked, 'thank you.'

'What do you mean, not too bad?' Mum said, quickly. 'Has it been hurting?'

'It twinged a bit this morning when I knelt down in assembly.'

'You be careful – you want it right for Thursday. Perhaps I ought to write a note and ask Miss Oxley to let you off games and that for the start of next week.'

'But I've got to practise,' Amy said. 'Anyway, Miss Oxley won't let me do anything I shouldn't. She says I'm the best chance we've got if Debra isn't better.'

'What's wrong with Debra?'

'She turned her ankle on the beam on Wednesday. She came down too heavy.'

Amy noticed that Richard was staring at her over the rim of his mug.

'*Kneeling?*' he said. 'In assembly?'

'Yes.'

'Hands - together - eyes - closed - Our - Father - which - art - in - heaven?'

'Yes.'

'Good God,' said Richard.

'What did *you* used to do in assembly, then?' Mum demanded, unfolding the ironing board. 'Stand on one leg?'

'We used to pass a marble up and down the back rows,' Richard said. 'The one who got caught with it lost. If you went through the whole term without getting nabbed you won the annual trophy. It was a conker in autumn,' he said.

'What, the trophy?'

'No, what we handed round. A marble in summer, a conker in autumn. It was sort of seasonal.'

'What was the trophy?' Amy asked, thinking of the Thames and Medway Inter-Schools Junior Gymnastic

Shield for which she and five others were to represent the school on Thursday evening.

'Oh, nothing you could cop hold of,' Richard said. 'Just the glory of knowing you'd got away with it. You ought to try it,' he suggested, 'but in the standing-up part. You'd never manage it during hands-together-eyes-closed.'

'You don't want to do anything of the sort,' Mum said, crossly.

She draped one of Richard's non-iron shirts, which he took on the road with him, over the board and began to iron it. 'Richard, have you put your clothes in the machine?'

'They're still in the cab,' Richard said. 'I'll fetch them in a moment – you won't be doing them till tomorrow, will you? Something for you there, too, Amy – and Helen.'

'You stay out of trouble,' Mum said, turning back to Amy. Amy shrugged. She was never in trouble.

'You fetch my washing in, you can collect the presents as well,' Richard said.

'I don't want her climbing about in that thing,' Mum said. She always called Richard's lorry a thing, as if calling it a lorry – or by its proper title, a Bedford TK – would make it undeservedly respectable. 'Go and get changed.'

'Me or – or – Mmmmm,' Amy said, looking at Richard.

'You, of course.'

Amy went upstairs. Her bedroom was at the front of the house, overlooking the road. From her window she could see the lorry stretching from one side of their front garden to the other. Richard had been her stepfather for six months and Mum had known him for longer than that before they married, but in all that time Amy had never set foot inside the lorry, front or back. It was not a place that she wanted to be in, anyway. The lorry was nothing to do with her, but she could hardly ignore it. The roof was on a level with her window and the front garden was so small that she felt that she might well be able to vault on to it, over the window sill. Richard referred to it as the office car when he came home in it. Mr Varley next door had a real office car, a Ford Escort Estate. Amy wished often that Richard's office car was something of that sort. He had a car of his own, but it was old and feeble, and spent a lot of time inside out on the wasteland by the garages.

Mum did not like seeing the lorry parked outside the house. 'Lumping great thing,' she said, complaining that it blocked the light. Later, Richard would take it back to the depot on the industrial estate and leave the box to be loaded up ready for Monday, while the cab came back with him and stayed over the weekend. Amy thought it was the oddest sight in the world, Richard's cab without the box attached, like a snail that had shed its shell and gone sprinting off without it.

While she was staring the front door opened and Richard came out into the garden below, heading for the lorry. She still felt a little surprised when she saw him, partly because he was away so much that she had never had time to become accustomed to his living there, and partly because he did not look like her idea of a lorry driver. She had always thought of lorry drivers as muscular hulks in boiler suits and flat caps, with enormous hands, and feet in enormous boots. Richard was only middling tall and quite lean, and all he wore on his head was his hair, fair and fine, rather like Helen's. Helen was not the only person who thought he was her father.

Amy's hair was like Mum's, dark brown, and springy.

Richard was now in the road, on the off-side of the cab,

climbing in. Amy could see him moving about awkwardly inside, like a rabbit in a hutch which it had outgrown. After a moment the door slammed and he reappeared on the pavement carrying his holdall full of dirty washing and a carrier bag which must contain the presents for herself and Helen, and for Mum. He brought back something for them every week and Amy knew that he enjoyed the moment when he would open the carrier and bring out his gifts, but she did not hurry downstairs when she heard him come indoors again. Instead she began to change very slowly out of her school shoes and to take off her uniform.

Mum called up the stairs, 'There's something for you down here!' She did not say, 'Come and see what Richard's brought you.' See, you don't know what to call him either, to me, Amy thought. She called back, 'I'll be down in a minute. I'm just changing.'

'He's got to take that thing back in a minute. Come now.'

'I'm hurrying,' Amy yelled, proceeding more slowly than ever. 'I've got my lace knotted.' This was the right thing to say. Mum was always annoyed if she took off her shoes without untying the laces. As she said it she pulled the wrong end of the bow with a vicious jerk and the lace went into a tight knot. It would take her ages to work it loose. After a bit she heard the lorry start up and grind away along the crescent, and at last it was safe to go down and see what Richard had brought her back from Up North, without having to decide how to say thank you. She wanted to thank him, very much, but she did not know how to.

When at last she did go down Mum was frowning over the ironing board and Helen was under the table playing with a woolly toy, Richard's present to her.

'Seal,' Helen said, holding it up for Amy to see. 'Daddy's seal.' On the window sill stood a new pot plant. Mum was not overfond of house plants because they collected dust and the leaves took ages to polish and they attracted insects, but either Richard had not discovered this yet or he was pretending not to notice. He liked plants very much, himself, and nearly always brought one back with him. The living room was full of them and in the back garden was an aluminium-framed greenhouse that had arrived in sections and was waiting for Richard to find time to fit them together. Amy's dad would have made his own, out of wood.

'That's yours,' Mum said, nodding toward the table. 'I don't know why you couldn't have come down for it before he left.'

'My *lace* was in a *knot*,' Amy growled and snaked her hand through the piles of clean ironing on the table top, to find her present, wrapped festively in coloured paper. Richard always did up his gifts nicely. Amy found it strange to imagine him sitting in his cab in a layby, somewhere in the North of England, wrapping up presents in fancy paper. She eased off the Sellotape carefully and looked inside. This week's offering was a pair of leg-warmers.

'There, now,' Mum said, driving the iron through the pile of a white towel like a snow plough, 'don't you wish you'd opened it while he was here?'

'Yes,' said Amy, trying to sound regretful, but she was not. She needed new leg-warmers urgently and Richard must have chosen these specially, but she would have been terribly embarrassed at having to say as much and so, she thought, would he.

Later on, after tea, while they were all watching television, she heard the lorry once more, returning without its box and being driven round to the open space by the garages. She ran upstairs, put on the leg-warmers and went down again to stand in the living room where Richard would not be able to help noticing her, and what she was wearing, but Mum noticed her first.

'What have you got them on for?'

'I just wanted to try them out,' Amy said.

'Don't be silly,' said Mum, 'you know what leg-warmers feel like. You want to keep them nice for gymnastics practice.'

'I want to wear them,' Amy said.

'Don't be such a baby. Put them away now or you'll catch them on something and then you'll have snags.'

Amy looked round at the living room. Thanks to Dad's love of a nice finish there was nothing on which she could possibly snag her leg-warmers, but she could not bring herself to explain to Mum that if Richard saw her wearing them he would know that she was pleased and then she would not have to say thank you. She went upstairs again, very slowly, and hung around at the bend, halfway up, but Richard must have lingered out by the garages, talking to a friend, for it was not until she was on her way down, without the leg-warmers, that he came in at the back door and met her in the hall.

He stopped there and she stopped too, on the third step from the bottom; there was a short silence.

'Thank you very much for my present,' Amy said, feet together, eyes closed. When she opened them again Richard was standing in the doorway of the living room, looking sad.

'I'm glad you like them. Do they fit?'

'Yes; thank you.'

'Not too long?'

'No. Thank you very much.'

Once, at school, they had had a visit from a real live author and Amy had had to get up at the end of her talk to thank her for coming. The real live author was famous, Amy had seen her on telly once, but it had been much easier to say thank you to her than it was to say thank you to Richard. In a way she had seemed more real and alive than he did, even though he was standing only a few feet away, and was not famous at all.

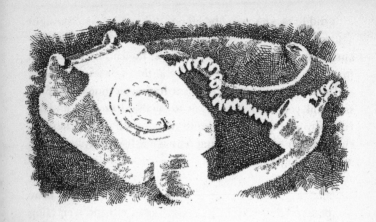

Chapter Two

Moving round the house on Saturday mornings was like one of those playground games where you had to creep and dodge and freeze suddenly. It was such a small house, even with only four of them in it, that it was almost impossible to move from one room to another without running into somebody. Amy and Richard evaded each other gamely for a couple of hours – Amy by tidying her bedroom and Helen's; Richard by hiding behind the *Daily Mirror* – until Richard gave up and took Helen to the swing park. Amy looked out of her window and watched them plodding down the road with Helen's wooden cart, made by Dad for the baby he had never seen, trailing behind them on a string. Richard's seal was rollicking unsteadily in the driving seat.

'You could have gone with them,' Mum said, when Amy came downstairs.

'Did you want some shopping done, then? I'll go now.'

'I didn't mean that,' Mum said. 'I just thought you might like to have . . .'

'I'll help you,' Amy said, miserably. She was even beginning to be polite to Mum. 'I'll do the hall.' She went to the cupboard under the stairs and fetched out the spray polish for the table, Windolene for the looking glass and the special anti-static cloth for the telephone. If you used an ordinary cloth the telephone mysteriously ended up dustier than it had been when you began. She saved the telephone until last, when all the other dust had settled, and was just reaching out to lift the receiver when it began to ring. Amy jumped back, horribly startled, feeling numb and trembling like the time when she had poked her finger into the toaster to see what would happen. For a moment she was too startled to answer it but Mum was out in the garden, putting the pedal bin sack into the dustbin, so she had to pick up the handset and whisper, 'Hullo?'

She whispered it so quietly that the party at the other end did not hear her.

'Hullo? Is anyone there? *Hullo!*'

'Gran!'

'Oh, Amy.' Gran sounded shaken, too. 'Is Susan there?'

'She's in the garden. How are you? I'm going to be in the gymnastics competition on Thursday – for the area trophy. Miss Oxley says –'

'Amy – can you fetch her?'

'She'll be in in a moment,' Amy said. 'If we win we might get chosen for the county team. Well, I don't suppose *I'll* be, and my knee's a bit dodgy, you know, where I twisted it that time, but Debra, she's my friend, my *other* friend –'

'Amy!' Gran's voice was unexpectedly sharp. 'Get your mum, quickly. Please.'

'Is something wrong?' Amy was alarmed. Gran was usually the easiest person to talk to and she never raised her voice.

'Yes – no – don't worry. Just call Susan in, there's a love.'

Amy put down the handset and ran into the garden, frightened. Gran was forty miles away, in Colchester, but her anxious, almost angry voice, was right there, in Amy's ear. Mum was by the fence, talking to Mrs Varley.

'. . . well, he rings every night, but you can't help wondering, especially when the weather's bad, high winds, *you* know, and that great box on the back –'

'Mum!'

'I've told you before not to interrupt,' Mum said. 'It's not nice manners.' Then she turned and saw Amy's face. 'What's the matter?'

'Gran – on the phone,' Amy said. 'I think something's happened.'

'Happened? What's happened?'

'I don't know. She just said to hurry.' Mum flapped her hands wildly at Mrs Varley and ran indoors. Amy stayed by the fence. Mrs Varley was not a nosy neighbour; she had no need to be because Mum told her everything, anyway; in fact she had known about Richard before Amy had and Amy had never quite forgiven her for this, but she felt that when Mum came out again, with what was now almost certain to be bad news, it would be a comfort to have Mrs Varley on hand to cushion the impact. She had been very kind when Dad died, Amy recalled and then, looking up at Mrs Varley, she realized what Gran's telephone call might mean.

'Grandad!' she said, and felt her hands flap, as Mum's had done.

'Now, then,' Mrs Varley said, firmly. 'Don't panic. You don't know *what* it is yet.'

'Grandad's ill.'

'How can you tell?' Mrs Varley leaned over the woven panel fence that Dad had put up and grasped her shoulder. 'You always meet trouble half-way, you and your mum. It mightn't be anything much.'

'He might be dead.'

'I don't suppose so. He's not very old, is he?'

Grandad was fifty-five. Amy thought that that was quite old enough to be dead. Dad had been only thirty. She began to feel really afraid, not at the thought of Grandad dying but of seeing Mum crying again. For the first time ever, but only for a moment, she wished that Richard were home.

'Well, don't stand there dithering,' Mrs Varley was saying. 'Go and find out.' Amy pulled away from under her hand and went into the house, slowly. Mum was in the hall, not doing anything, holding the telephone receiver down with one hand as though she had forgotten to let go of it, and pressing the other against her head. She was standing absolutely still. Amy did not know what to say or do, and it was with enormous relief that she saw Richard and Helen loom up on the other side of the reed glass panel in the front door.

Richard was very calm, but then it was not his father who was in hospital, having an emergency operation. Richard's parents lived in Canada, with his married sister and her family. Amy knew them only as smiles in photographs.

'He's on the danger list,' Mum kept saying, and Amy, in spite of her fright, was impressed. She had heard of the danger list before and imagined it to be a kind of national register of extremely ill people. She wondered how ill you had to be to get on it.

Richard went back into the hall and telephoned the railway station to check timetables because the car, which they had not been expecting to need this weekend, was round at the garage having something urgent done to its gearbox.

Mum ran upstairs to fetch a suitcase and ran down again. 'Can't you get it back?'

Richard, on the telephone, was trying to hold two conversations at once. 'What about two-thirty?' he said. 'Is there one from Liverpool Street – no, I can't. It's in bits – from Liverpool Street at around half past ... half past exactly? Gets in at three-twenty ... I see. Thank you.' He hung up. 'I looked in on the way home from the park. Dennis started on it this morning. I can't go and tell him to shove it all back, can I?'

'How'm I going to get to the station?'

'I'll run you down in the cab. Look, why *don't* you leave Helen here? With me and Amy?'

'No – no, I can manage Helen.' Mum turned on the bottom stair and ran up again. Amy heard her thumping about in the bedroom, sorting clothes. Very slowly it began to dawn on her that as long as Mum was away in Colchester, there would have to be rearrangements. She waited until Richard had finished scribbling on the pad by the telephone and said, 'What's going to happen to me?'

'We're staying here,' Richard said, still calm. Too calm, Amy thought.

'Just us? Can't I go with Mum?'

'Better not,' Richard said.

'I wouldn't be in the way.' Amy realized, with mounting

panic, that if she did not go with Mum she would be left alone with Richard for the weekend.

'Well, you would, rather,' Richard said, tactlessly.

'But Helen's going – it's not fair.'

'Not fair? Good grief, this isn't a holiday!' Richard cried, forgetting to be polite, for once. 'They aren't going for fun.'

'Then why can't Helen stay here?'

'She's too little. Susan would worry, and she's got enough to worry about, right now.'

'If I went I could help look after her. I used to when – when – before . . .' Amy was going to say, 'Before you came,' and wanted to add, 'And if you weren't here, I'd *have* to go.'

Richard seemed to know what she was thinking.

'We'll be all right on our own. I can cook, you know.'

'But –' Amy had another idea. 'Suppose Mum isn't back tomorrow – I mean, if Grandad . . . if, if . . . I mean, you'll be off Up North again on Monday.'

Mum, on her way downstairs, heard that.

'Oh, Amy, do stop making trouble. If I can't get back in time Richard will stay at home.'

'Or,' Richard said, 'Amy could come with me.'

'What, in the lorry?' Amy said, aghast.

'Why not? A lot of drivers take their kids on trips.'

But I'm not your kid, Amy thought.

Mum said, 'Of course she can't go with you. She can't miss school.'

'She's entitled to a fortnight's holiday during term time. Everyone is.'

Who said it wasn't a holiday, then? Amy mouthed silently, at his back. 'But I've got the gymnastics on Thursday.'

'That's right. She's got the gymnastics.' Mum went into the kitchen.

'You wouldn't mind missing the gymnastics, would you?' Richard asked. Amy gaped at him, incredulous and outraged. 'It would give your knee a chance to mend,' he added, pointedly.

'I've got to go. Miss Oxley said I'm our only hope if Debra's ankle isn't better.'

Mum looked out of the kitchen doorway and frowned at Richard. 'We'll talk about that later. Can you see to Helen? She needs changing.'

Richard glanced over his shoulder as he followed her. 'If you went to Colchester you might not be back in time for Thursday, had you thought of that?'

'Then why can't I go to Colchester?'

He turned, came back into the hall, and stood very squarely in front of her.

'Amy, for God's sake stop being difficult. Your grandad's ill and your gran's all on her own. Susan's half out of her mind with worry. Grow up, can't you? You're the last person we need to be worrying about at the moment.'

This was so unlike Richard, so rude and so decisive, that Amy was lost for a retort. Richard stumped into the kitchen and she went up to her room and sat on the bed, staring at her black leotard, beautifully pressed by Mum and hung on a coat hanger with the scarlet hairband looped round the hook and the new leg-warmers folded over the cross bar.

'I *won't* miss Thursday,' Amy said, through her teeth, and imagined herself in a comic strip, running away and hiding so that Richard could not force her to come Up North with him and miss the Vital Competition. She wasn't even too sure where Up North was. Near the top, somewhere, wasn't it, just before Scotland? All she knew was that when Richard was Up North he wasn't here. Up North was somewhere else, a place for Richard to be. How could she possibly be there too?

'You're coming to the station to see me off?' Mum said, emerging at last with the filled suitcase. Richard was sitting on the third step from the bottom of the stairs, packing Helen into her coat and tights.

'There won't be room,' Amy said, 'not in the cab.' This was true, but if she had wanted to go she would have argued ferociously that there would be plenty of room if they all squeezed up.

'There'll be room if we all squeeze up,' Mum said, looking hurt.

'Not with the suitcase,' said Amy. She had sworn a solemn oath, up in the bedroom, that she was not going anywhere in the lorry, ever, and now seemed as good a time as any to put it into practice. 'I'll stay here – someone might phone.'

'Why should they? It doesn't matter if they do,' Mum said.

'Gran might.'

'No she won't. I've just rung her to say that Susan's on her way – you know that,' Richard said. He spoke without looking up, without, as far as Amy could tell, moving his lips. He was angry, angrier than she had ever seen him before. He sometimes came home from a trip in a bad mood about the customers, or the foreman at the depot, but they were things that belonged somewhere else, Up North, Down Town, and as soon as he had relieved his feelings, usually under his breath, he forgot about them. Now he was angered by something that was happening in the house, that could not be left behind or shut out. He squashed Helen's fat hands into her mittens and looked up at Mum.

'Let her stay here if she wants. We shan't be gone long. I'll go and get the cab round.' He went out. Mum picked up Helen and looked over her head at Amy.

'Don't be upset, pet. I expect Grandad will be all right. I'll ring as soon as I get there.'

Amy had forgotten about Grandad and his operation.

'I *can't* miss the gymnastics. I don't want to go Up North.'

'Of course you're not going Up North,' Mum said. 'He only said that on the spur of the moment.'

'But *he* doesn't want to stop here,' Amy said. 'He won't want to lose a week's money, will he?'

'That's none of your business – and stop calling him "he",' Mum said, unfairly. 'There's his thing – are you sure you don't want to come?'

Amy shook her head. Mum shrugged. 'Well, be a good girl. I might be back in a day or two.' She leaned over and kissed Amy on the cheek. Helen poked her in the eye, aimlessly, and said, 'Eye,' with a clever smile.

'Aren't you going to wish me luck?' Amy said.

'Wish you luck?'

'For the gymnastics.'

'Of course – good luck – but I expect I'll be back by then.' Richard came in from the street, picked up the suitcase and went out again without looking at Amy. Mum followed him, waved from the step, and closed the door behind her.

Amy sat on the stairs, where Richard had sat, and watched the oddly wavering figures bob down the path, through the distorting glass in the door. There were scrambled movements at a distance as Richard helped Mum to climb up into the cab, the nearside door slammed, then the driver's door; then the glass, which had been stained blue by the lorry's paintwork, cleared once more as the vehicle drove off.

Amy stayed where she was. It would take fifteen minutes to reach the station, fifteen minutes to wait for the train to London, if it arrived on time, and fifteen minutes home again. In less than an hour Richard would be back in the house and there they would be, imprisoned together for the rest of the weekend and perhaps longer.

Suppose Grandad – well, suppose Mum didn't get back in a day or two. She would have to get up every morning and find Richard in the kitchen, boiling eggs and making toast. She would come home from school and find Richard preparing the tea. It would be Richard who did the shopping and she was sure he would do it badly because he would not know how much anything cost, or where to go for good bargains and they would run out of money and be reduced to borrowing from Mrs Varley who had hard things to say about people who borrowed money. Richard would have to do the washing and ironing and she knew what he thought about ironing. The housework would not get done and the place would look mucky and Mum would be furious when she did get back. Amy's mind sprinted ahead to Thursday.

Mum had planned to leave Helen with Mrs Varley for the afternoon because Mrs Varley, who worked at the wool shop by the library, had early closing on Thursdays, and take the bus over to Chatham for the gymnastics competition. They had decided to have tea out afterwards. She wondered if Richard would come instead or would he be sulking too at having to stay at home? If the car wasn't ready he might turn up in the cab, and she would have to go home with him in it. But they might need the cab at the depot for the relief driver and if the car hadn't been repaired they would have to get buses everywhere. Richard never caught buses and knew nothing about timetables. Amy imagined him arriving late at the competition, climbing over people's laps to find a seat and fatally distracting someone who was performing perilous exercises on the beam while Amy cringed in a corner and pretended that he was nothing to do with her.

It was growing chilly in the hall. Amy stood up, stanched the two or three tears on her face, and slouched into the kitchen which was just as Mum had left it when she went to put the rubbish in the dustbin and the telephone had rung. It was a mess, abandoned halfway through its weekly clean-up. Amy put a fresh liner in the pedal bin and plugged in the Hoover that Mum had left ready in the middle of the floor. She was on a chair, stretching across the sink to wipe the window sill when Richard finally came home, and she noticed that he had been away an hour and twenty minutes. She heard him call from the front door, 'Put the grill on, Amy – warm a couple of plates.'

He sounded quite cheerful. She had been afraid that he would come back as angry as he had been when he left, but he bounced into the kitchen waving a little white carrier bag.

'Chinese takeaway,' he said, holding it up. 'Save time till we get ourselves sorted out.'

Amy sighed deeply as she reached over to switch on the grill. Chinese takeaway: the rot was setting in already.

Chapter Three

Amy could not remember a weekend when they had watched so much television. They watched everything, beginning with sport on Saturday afternoon while they ate the Chinese meal, on their laps, in the living room. She had never had a Chinese meal before and she had never eaten, no one *ever* ate, in the living room. Mum had shampooed the carpet only the previous week, and Amy watched fearfully in case Richard splashed sweet and sour sauce on it or lost intractable slippery bean shoots down the side of the settee. She was so concerned about what was happening on Richard's plate that she did not notice what was going on under her own spoon and fork until a crisp-fried pork ball rolled off the plate and bounced under the coffee table. Richard was staring at the screen and did not see her retrieve it, and being so crisp it did not leave a mark, but she went hot when she thought what a mess it might have made, had it been anywhere near the sweet and sour sauce before it escaped. After that she finished as quickly as possible, put her plate on the table and watched the football, all the while waiting for the telephone to ring.

By five there was still no word from Colchester.

'D'you think we ought to ring *her*?' Amy said.

'Better not,' said Richard. 'She'll ring when she's ready.'

They had tea in front of the television too, and then watched it all evening.

'This is a load of old rope,' Richard said, from time to time. 'Shall we try something else?'

'Yes, if you like,' Amy said courteously.

They turned to Channel 4, then to BBC 2.

'Are you enjoying this?' Richard said, after a bit.

'I don't mind. Are you?' Amy said.

'Not a lot – shall we switch over?'

'Yes.'

'Are you sure?'

'Yes.'

'Certain?'

'If you are.'

Richard turned to Southern and said, 'Oh no, I draw the line –' Then he said, 'What about you?'

'I don't mind.'

'Do you like quiz programmes?'

'Yes – but I don't like them *much*.'

'I can't stand this one,' Richard said. 'But if you want it –'

'Oh no, not if you don't.'

'Just say.'

'No. It's all right.'

They turned to BBC 1 again. The programme had moved on and there was a film. They sat and watched it but as they had missed the all-important first twenty minutes it was hard to tell what was happening.

'Can you make any of this out?' Richard asked her, after a while.

'Not really.'

'D'you want to stick with it?'

'If you do.'

'No, I'm asking *you*.'

'I don't mind.'

They persevered with the film which became stranger and stranger and less and less intelligible and, after a bit, quite rude, Amy thought. Fancy putting it on so early. But while they were looking at the television they did not have to look at each other, and while they were listening they did not have to talk. The tea plates remained on the floor, unwashed. Amy saw how easy it was to let yourself go.

At half past seven the telephone rang. Richard went to answer it and Amy seized the opportunity to clear away the plates. She put on the kettle too, for coffee, and filled the basin in the sink with hot water. Richard came in as she was squeezing washing-up liquid over the plates.

'That was Susan,' Richard said. 'She says your grandad's had his operation and they think he's going to be all right but your gran's a bit upset – well, she's very upset,' he amended, catching Amy's eye, 'and Susan's going to stay for a few days until they're sure everything's OK.'

'She won't be back by Thursday, then?' Amy said. To save facing him she put on Mum's rubber gloves and plunged her hands into the basin. The gloves were too large and the water clamped them hotly against her fingers. It was as if some creature had been lurking in the bowl, under the bubbles, and grabbed her hands in a toothless mouth.

'I wouldn't bank on it,' Richard said. He picked up the Fairy Liquid bottle. 'Look, have you ever done this?' He pressed it gently and a jet of tiny bubbles shot up towards the ceiling, glinting exquisitely in the light of the fluorescent tube. 'Isn't it pretty?'

'Mmmm,' Amy said. Richard tilted the bottle to bring more liquid into the neck and wastefully did it again. 'It leaves little sticky marks,' said Amy.

'It's good news about your grandad,' Richard said. 'Isn't it?' Amy took a cloth and wiped away the splashes where the bubbles were bursting against the window pane. 'Shall I make coffee?'

'If you'd like some.'

'I would. Would you?'

'Yes please.'

Amy stacked the clean plates in the rack, swilled out the bowl and began to dry up. Richard stretched out an eager hand to help her put the crockery away and dashed a mug against the side of the sink. It broke into several shards and Richard was left holding the handle.

'That was Mum's favourite,' Amy said.

'I know – I gave it to her,' Richard said, regretfully, meaning perhaps that he knew where he could get another. But Amy, furious at his clumsiness, did not stop to think what he had meant.

'It's still her favourite,' she snapped, and did not realize, until she saw his face, bent over the fragments, what a nasty thing it was to have said.

*

She went up to bed at half past nine. Usually there was an argument about this on Saturdays but tonight she went punctually and could not help noticing that Richard had switched off the television before she reached the top of the stairs. Already the house was different. The door of Helen's room was shut. It was always left ajar in case Helen called out in the night, but Helen was in Colchester, sleeping in Mum's old cot that Gran still kept for their visits. Amy had herself slept in it when she was a baby. Mum would be in the back bedroom that had been hers when she lived with Gran and Grandad and had been Susan Shenstone. Richard had never been to Colchester, for Gran did not like Richard much; Amy had heard her say things. She went to bed and lay staring at her leotard where it hung in the beam of the street lamp, and muttering her vow until she went to sleep. She was not, definitely not, going Up North with Richard, not on Monday, not ever.

When she got up in the morning she looked out of the bathroom window and saw him at the end of the garden, clearing a rectangular patch of earth among the weeds that Dad would never have allowed to grow so tall. He must have been at it for some time for although it was still only twenty past eight he had very nearly completed the job. When he had finished he moved away and stood looking purposefully at the prefabricated slices of greenhouse. Evidently he intended to spend the day in the garden. Amy wondered what they would do about lunch and if the Chinese takeaway was open on Sundays.

She managed to keep herself busy round the house for a couple of hours, first tidying up, then putting in some gymnastics practice in the living room, with the furniture pushed well back, wearing her old leotard and the super-annuated leg-warmers. Occasionally she was aware of a distant clatter from the garden and when at last she went into the kitchen to put on the kettle for elevenses she saw Richard in the middle of the lawn surrounded by the sections of the greenhouse, laid out like an enormous tangram. He did not appear to be making very much progress and seemed discouraged, standing there with the greenhouse in bits all round him. The sun had gone in and Amy felt sorry for him, almost, lurking out in the cold drizzle when he could have been indoors by the fire which he had thoughtfully lit in the living room before he went out. She tapped on the window and held out the coffee jar.

Richard turned warily at the sound, saw the jar and nodded with enthusiasm. He's overdoing it a bit, Amy remarked, as he came in rubbing his hands, until she saw that his fingers were purple and stiff with cold. The thought, This place isn't big enough for both of us, went through her mind; there was more room with four of them in it.

'I'll just go up and wash,' Richard said, and as he spoke someone rang the doorbell. He went to answer it on his way upstairs and after a moment Debra came into the kitchen. Amy noticed with alarm that she was not limping.

'Where's your mum?' Debra asked, looking round. 'I saw her going off in the lorry yesterday.'

'My grandad's ill in Colchester,' Amy said. 'He's on the danger list. She's gone up to stay with Gran. She took Helen. There's just me and . . . and . . . Mmmm.' She looked down at Debra's feet in their wobbling high-heeled shoes. 'Your ankle better?'

'Yes. My mum took me down the doctor's last night. He said if I'm careful and keep the bandage on I'll be all right.'

34

'All right for Thursday?'

'Yes, if I'm careful.'

Richard came in just at the wrong moment, to Amy's way of thinking, and overheard her.

'That's good news, isn't it?'

Debra beamed at him. 'I thought I wouldn't be able to be in it but it's all right now.'

Amy frowned into the coffee jar and measured out spoonfuls. 'D'you want some?'

'Can I just have milk? It's better for you, isn't it, when you're training.'

Amy felt light-minded and emptied her own coffee back into the jar.

'Training?' said Richard.

'Yes, for Thursday. Just milk, I'm having, and only salads and that. But we'll have burgers on Thursday, after.'

'Salads? At this time of year? Sooner you than me,' Richard said and he looked disapproving. 'You're not on a diet, are you?' he asked Amy.

'Mum was making me salads last week,' Amy said.

'I suppose that Chinese meal ruined everything, then.'

'Oh, Chinese is all right – I expect,' Debra said, generously. 'It's not got much carbohydrates in it, I don't expect. I mean, it's mostly sort of cooked salad, anyway.'

'OK, we'll have fried salad for lunch, then,' Richard said.

Now *he* was being light-minded. Amy handed him his coffee mug and said primly, 'What *are* we having for lunch?'

'Toasted lettuce?' Richard suggested. 'Roast cucumber? Steamed radishes?'

'No, really.'

'I hadn't thought about it,' Richard admitted. 'Can't we open a tin?'

'What tin?'

'There's a steak and kidney pudding in the cupboard.'

'That's for emergencies.'

'This is an emergency.'

'I thought you said you could cook.'

They all laughed. Amy, bending to put the milk bottle back in the fridge, was shaken. How could they be laughing and making jokes, she and Richard? They never did. It must be because of Debra. She looked over her shoulder. 'Can Debra stay to lunch?'

'What, and eat steak and kidney pudding?' Richard said, pretending to be shocked. 'It'll weigh her down like concrete on Thursday.'

'I don't suppose a tin will stretch to three,' Debra said, tactfully. 'Mum's expecting me home, anyway.'

Amy made her milk last as long as possible and hoped that Debra would do the same, but before she was half-way down the mug Debra had finished and was looking at her watch.

'I'd better be going,' Debra said, heading for the kitchen door. Amy followed her into the hall.

'You don't have to go yet, do you?'

'I'd better,' Debra said. She looked uneasy.

'What d'you come for, then? You've only been here five minutes.'

'Seven.' Debra looked at her watch again. 'I just come to tell you about my ankle.' She moved to the front door. Amy leaned on it.

'You can stay a bit. Come upstairs.'

'No, really. I got to go.' She pulled the door open against Amy's weight, and began to edge out. 'I expect your mum'll be back soon.'

So that's it! Amy thought, angrily banging the door behind her. She doesn't like it either with just Richard here. She was about to go up to her room but Richard called from the kitchen: 'Amy! Here a minute.'

She went in, cautiously.

'So Debra's going to be all right for Thursday,' Richard said. He was rinsing the mugs, ostentatiously tidy and with exaggerated caution.

'Yes.' Amy was on her guard at once.

'So it won't matter too much if you're not there?'

'Yes it will. I can't just not turn up.'

'You could if there were extenuating circumstances.'

'You what?'

'If there was a good reason for not turning up.'

'But there isn't.'

'Well . . . there is. Sit down, Amy.' He seated himself at the table. 'Amy, sit down, I want to talk to you.'

Amy sat down. For the first time since Saturday morning they faced each other. 'Susan said you thought I might be worried at losing a week's money if I had to stay at home with you.'

'Yes,' Amy said. She relaxed. It was going to be all right. She looked again at Richard's face. No it wasn't.

'Well, you were right. Sorry, Amy, but we can't afford it, not with the car being done – and the phone bill.'

'Haven't we got any saved?' She felt daring. She would never have said that to Mum.

'Of course, but not much, and even the train fare to Colchester makes a difference. We weren't expecting that, you see.'

'Oh.'

'You know what I'm trying to say, don't you?'

37

'No,' Amy said, unhelpfully. She remembered her oath and crossed her fingers under the table to reinforce it.

'Look, Amy, I know you want to go to that competition, but you're only the reserve, aren't you?'

'I'm not *only* the reserve,' Amy cried angrily. 'If Debra hadn't been all right –'

'But she *is* all right.'

'Only if she's careful.'

'I reckon she'll be careful. Diets . . .'

'But someone else may be away.'

'You, for instance. Look, if you're only needed if someone else is away, you're the reserve.'

'But I'm supposed to *be* there,' Amy shouted. She was suddenly inspired, recalling yesterday's sport on television. 'What about football? The reserves have to go to the match.'

'That's not the same thing.'

'Yes it is.'

'Amy, it isn't.' Richard put his arms on the table and leaned across it, earnestly. 'Spurs v. Man United with a gate of thousands and millions of viewers isn't the same as me losing a week's wages in *case* you're needed for half an hour on Thursday. You must see that.'

Amy, first and second fingers already crossed, folded third over fourth and yelped with cramp.

'What on earth are you doing?' Richard said. 'Come on, Amy, it's not just the gymnastics, is it? You don't *want* to come with me, do you?'

Amy looked at her lap and made the noncommittal noises she always used for him.

'You'd like it, I'm sure you would. I wanted to take you on a trip in the Christmas holidays but Susan said no, because the traffic would be bad and there was fog.'

'I don't want to go if Mum doesn't want me to,' Amy said.

'She'll understand.'

'Are you going to ring her up and say?'

'Tomorrow.'

'Why not now?'

'Tomorrow will do,' Richard said, shiftily.

'After we start.'

'Yes, from London.'

'When it's too late for her to say no,' Amy snapped. 'That's not fair.'

'I don't want to worry her,' Richard said. 'I can't take a holiday because I had this year's time early, when we got married. Cars and phones and washing machines cost money. I *need* this week's work – anyway, there's something I want to show you.'

'Where?' Amy looked around.

'Not here. In Oldham.'

'Where's Oldham? London?'

'London! Don't you do geography at school?'

'Not much. We're doing ancient Egypt at the moment.'

'That's history.'

'Egypt's still there,' Amy pointed out.

'All right. So it is. Look, hang about.' He jumped up.

'Where are you going?'

'Just out to the cab – to fetch my maps.' He was out of the door before she could say anything, and running down the back garden path. In amazement she saw him leap over the gate, only one hand on the concrete post to steady himself. A few minutes later he came back the same way but this time he had a long hardboard box under his arm.

'I didn't know you could vault,' Amy said.

39

'Wait till you see me up and down off that tailgate,' Richard said. Amy had no intention of seeing him do anything on the tailgate, whatever it might be. He put the box on the table and leafed expertly through it. It was half a metre long and packed with maps. 'Ah, this is it.' He took out one of the maps and unfolded it.

'There's not room in here,' Amy said. 'Let's do it in the front – I pushed all the furniture out of the way – for my warm-up,' she added, sulkily. Richard took no notice. He followed her into the living room with the map crackling in his hands like a starched tablecloth. He knelt on the floor, spread out the map, and motioned Amy to come down beside him.

'Now, do you see where this is?'

'London?' Amy said. The map was writhing with roads and there was no coastline to give her a clue.

'Forget London. We shan't even stop there –'

'Except to phone Mum.'

'Except to phone. This is Lancashire. Look – there's Manchester, and here's Huddersfield.'

'Do you go to Manchester?'

'Sometimes – I think it'll be Stockport this week. That's Stockport. Now, can you find Oldham?'

It struck Amy that Richard would make a very good teacher, tricking you into finding things out for yourself instead of teaching you. She forgot her sulk and craned her neck over the map. If this was Up North, it was a mess.

'There.'

'That's right. Now, see this road, out through Oldham and Rochdale, that's where the mills are.'

'Windmills?' Once, when she and Mum had gone to stay with Gran, when Helen was born, Grandad had taken her out for the day. They had driven up to Norfolk and she remembered the windmills, standing among flat fields.

'No, cotton mills.'

'Is that where they make cotton?' In spite of what he had said a hazy picture began to form of a windmill with a huge spool on a spindle sticking out from the hub of its vanes. The vanes began to turn and white cotton, hundreds and thousands of metres of it, unwound from the spool as if on a gigantic sewing machine.

'They used to. Most of them are empty now, or used for something else. They've all got names.'

'Names? What, like Cranbrook Mill and that?'

'No, not like that. Cranbrook Mill's in Cranbrook. These are proper names – like Mona and Dawn and Coral.'

'Why?'

'I don't know. I never used to think about it much but just after I met your mum – and you – I saw one with your name on it.'

'A mill called Amy?'

'That's right, between Oldham and Rochdale. I was so surprised. It's a sign, I thought.'

Amy ignored that, guessing what he meant.

'Why's it called Amy?'

'I don't know. We could find out. But I always thought you'd like to see it. There aren't many people with a mill named after them. We could take a photo – you and the mill.'

'Mmmmm,' said Amy.

'Well, what about it?'

'Will we really see it? You're not just saying?'

'Of course we will. I don't know the actual route yet, until I've seen the order forms, but if we can't pass it in the lorry we'll make a special trip.'

'What do they look like?'

'The mills? Like big factories – hundreds of windows. But they've all got a tower on the end and that's where the names are written up. White on red brick. It's very dark red brick up there.'

'Dirty,' Amy said.

'No – just dark.'

Amy tried to imagine them but all she could see still were windmills, like they had in Norfolk, with AMY painted on the side in huge white letters. There was something threatening about them, a sense of menace and imminent danger, as if they concealed something not nice, but she could not think why until they were folding the map away, and then she remembered a hymn that they sometimes sang at school: dark satanic mills.

'There might be fog,' she said.

Chapter Four

'There might be frost,' Amy said. 'Black ice.'

'Not very likely,' Richard said, calmly, 'at the beginning
of April.' He was feeling pleased with himself because he
had remembered to do his washing.

It was Sunday evening and they were packing, ready for
an early start next day. 'But it'll be cold at night,' Richard
warned her. 'Just a nighty won't do. You'd better pack
bedsocks too.'

'Where are we sleeping, then?'

'In the box,' said Richard.

'In the box!'

'You know what the box is,' Richard said. 'The Luton
– the trailer. You've heard me talk about it, you must
have.'

'But . . . sleeping in it . . .'

'They give us an allowance on the road for bed and

breakfast, but it's so small a lot of us don't bother with it. We take it, all right, but we don't try and use it.'

'Isn't the box full of furniture?'

'It will be when we start but we'll have delivered a lot by the time we stop for the night. It'll be Cheltenham, probably, the first night. They have very superior public lavatories in Cheltenham.'

Amy, growing more alarmed, looked up from her packing.

'Public toilets?'

'We shall need them. I haven't got a bathroom in the box.'

'You mean, we have to *use* them – for washing and – and . . .' She knew that Richard used them. She had never thought of having to use them herself.

'Only in the mornings. There aren't many people about when I get up – it's quite private. At night I'll boil up a kettle on my stove and you can wash in the box. Oh yes, and you'd better put a hot water bottle in, too. You'll need it.'

'What am I going to sleep on?' Amy said.

'Camp bed, like I do,' said Richard. 'I'm borrowing one from Linda Varley. I've got to pick it up later tonight – Bob's getting it down from the loft.'

'Did you tell her why you needed it?'

'Of course.' Richard glanced up, warily.

'What did she say?'

He looked her in the eye. 'She doesn't approve. Nor do you – I can see.'

Amy muttered, 'I never knew we'd have to sleep in the box . . . public toilets . . .'

'Have you got a sponge bag?'

'What for?'

'What do you usually put in a sponge bag?'

'I didn't think we'd be needing toothpaste and flannels and things.'

'Oh, come *on*, Amy.' He angrily zipped up his travelling bag. 'I suppose you think I just give myself a quick wipe down with an oily rag. We're going to wash and clean our teeth and comb our hair, just like always.'

'In a public toilet?'

'I'm going to get that bed from Bob Varley,' Richard said, and went out quickly. Amy sat on the settee and poked about in her own bag. Then she went up to the bathroom, unhooked her hot water bottle from behind the door and collected her sponge bag from the cupboard by the basin. She had used it only once before, last summer, when she and Debra had gone on a weekend school trip to Brighton. Before that she had always used Mum's. From the bedroom she fetched Elizabeth, her balding and exhausted teddy bear who no longer actually slept with Amy but hung around the bedroom looking hurt and sometimes, when Amy was feeling miserable, dossed down under the pillow. Amy thought that Elizabeth might be consoling company during the long chilly nights in the box in a lorry park somewhere Up North.

Downstairs Richard came crashing in again with the bed. She heard him dump it in the hall and then came a tuneless clanging in the hot water pipes which meant that he was rearranging the half dried clothes on the kitchen radiator. He had forgotten to do his laundry until lunchtime and it had all come out in pale blue streaks because a sock had strayed into the washing machine. Amy was very glad that none of her own clothes had been in with it.

When she came down with the sponge bag, and Elizabeth concealed under her sweater, Richard was in the living room, tuning the television. He turned as Amy came in and stooped to put her sponge bag in her holdall.

'Don't pack that now,' he said, 'you'll need your things tonight.' She took it out again, crossly. She had not thought of that and was rather annoyed that he should have thought of it himself.

'What happens if we have an accident?'

'Why should we have an accident?'

'Well, motorway pile-ups and things like that.'

'It's possible,' Richard said, 'but on the whole you're better off in the cab of a lorry than anywhere else.'

'But I've seen pictures – that last bad winter there were pictures of lorries with their fronts all smashed up –'

'It's not winter!' Richard bellowed. 'It's spring. Anyway, I've seen you crossing The Runway. You'll be a sight safer in my cab than you are on your own two feet.'

'I always look both ways.'

'There's not much point in looking both ways if you don't take any notice of what you see. I nearly ran you over one morning. You never noticed.'

Amy scowled and took things out of her bag and put them in again.

'Anyway, you'd better get to bed,' Richard said. 'Early start tomorrow. I leave the depot at eight and I'll be back here for you at quarter past. I want you ready and waiting.'

'Aren't I coming to the depot with you?' Amy asked.

'Better not. We're doing this on the QT.'

'You mean, it's *illegal*?'

'Not that, so much, but the firm wouldn't approve.'

'Suppose they find out?'

'They won't find out.'

'But suppose we *do* crash? And the police come and – and –'

'If we're dead,' Richard said cheerfully, 'it won't matter if we get found out, will it? Now, go to bed. I've got to write that note to your teacher, what's her name?'

'Miss Oxley. She won't half go *on* . . .'

Amy scuffled towards the door. As she went out Richard said, 'Do you know what a pessimist is?'

'No.'

'Look in the mirror, then.'

'Me?'

'Yes, *you*. Gripe, gripe, gripe. Anyone'd think we were going to cross the Alps on roller skates.'

'Mrs Varley says I meet trouble half-way,' Amy said, scowling at him, and at the party wall behind which Mr and Mrs Varley were sitting, watching 'Mastermind'. She could hear it over the sound of their own set.

'Half-way?' Richard said. 'You don't meet trouble half-way, you go and knock on the door and yell through the letterbox, "Yoohoo, Trouble. Come on out. I've got a job for you!" '

When Richard had left in the morning Amy sat at the foot of the stairs, third step from the bottom, waiting for him to come back with the lorry and staring longingly at the telephone. It was almost eight o'clock. Richard had left at seven in order to make a detour and deliver his message to the school – where Amy's name would shortly be mud – and he would be back by quarter past eight, he had said.

As soon as he had gone Amy had washed up, made the beds, watered the plants and circled the house twice, ensuring that all the plugs were pulled from their sockets. That had taken thirty-five minutes. Since she had finished she had been here in the hall, gazing at the telephone. First of all she had hoped only that it would ring and that Mum would be on the other end, but after a while she began to think that it would be so easy to stretch out her hand and dial Gran's number in Colchester.

Mum, Richard's making me go Up North with him. I shall miss the gymnastics.

Mum would surely be angry about the gymnastics. In a way she was even more enthusiastic about the competition than Amy was. She would say, *Of course you can't go Up North. Tell Richard I want to talk to him. Tell him to ring me as soon as he gets in.*

That part was all right, but the part where Richard did get in, about fifteen minutes from now, Amy thought, looking at her watch, was not all right at all.

She had seen, over the last couple of days, that quiet, polite Richard had a rotten temper. It was not a short temper, but it was bad when you got to it. She could not even begin to guess at what he would say if he came back with the lorry and discovered that she had gone complaining to Mum. Debra did that all the time. 'Mum, I want . . . Mum, can I have . . .?' If Debra's mum said no, Debra went straight to her father. 'Dad, I want . . . Dad, can I have . . .?' Her timing was faultless. She didn't give them a chance to compare notes and as they rarely agreed about anything – even, on one memorable occasion, which side of the road to walk on – she usually got what she wanted from one or the other. Amy had never done that when her own dad was alive and it occurred to her now that it might be unwise to start on Richard.

She sat on the stairs and remembered Debra's mum and dad storming up The Runway one Saturday morning, bawling at each other from pavement to pavement, while their five children dodged back and forward through the traffic, unsure whose side it was wiser to be on.

The familiar churning, gravelly sound of the lorry's engine advanced along the crescent and the glass of the front door turned a quivering blue until Richard shut off the engine. Amy gathered up her bag and opened the door as Richard came up the path.

'Ready?'

'Yes,' Amy said, heavily.

'Back door locked? Water off? Gas off? Electricity off?'

'You did all that.'

'Just making sure.'

'Electricity's on because of the freezer,' Amy told him, 'but I pulled all the other plugs out.'

'Come on, then.'

'Aren't *you* going to check?'

'But you just said you'd done it.'

'I'd rather you checked.'

'D'you think I don't trust you?' Richard said.

'But you didn't *ask* me. I just did it.'

'I know,' Richard said. 'You're a good girl. Thank you very much.'

'I didn't mean that. Oh *please*,' Amy begged, with visions of the house blowing up in their absence, or burglars effecting an entry through a neglected window, floods, short circuits, Mrs Varley's cat shut in the bathroom and slowly starving.

'All right,' Richard said, stepping over the threshold.

'I'll have a look round. You get in the cab – I've left the door open.'

Amy hefted her bag and approached the lorry, but when she reached the cab, with its open door, there seemed to be no way of getting in. It had a step, but the step was on a level with her shoulder. The cab loomed. Amy threw her bag in but it hit the seat and bounced out again. She looked over her shoulder to see if Richard had reappeared but there was no sign of him. Rather than attempt an undignified scramble and end up falling out again, like the bag, she sauntered up and down the kerb to the end of the lorry and back, surveying the exposed parts under the box.

'What *are* you doing?' Richard asked, coming up behind her.

'Measuring it.' Amy jumped.

'Measuring it? How?'

'With my feet. They showed us at school.'

'I'd have thought there were easier ways. Don't you have rulers? How long do you make it?'

'Thirteen metres.'

'What's that in feet?'

'We don't use feet.'

'You were using *your* feet.'

'Not that sort of foot,' Amy said.

'Well, you're wrong, anyway,' Richard said, annoyingly. 'A metre's more than a yard and it's twelve yards long, head to tail.'

'Have you measured it?'

'Thirty-six feet's maximum for rigid vehicles.'

'Rigid?'

'All in one piece. When it goes round corners it doesn't articulate. Artics can be much longer.'

Amy had thought that the artic was the place at the top of the world where the North Pole was, as far Up North as you could be. Perhaps an artic was a kind of travelling fridge for frozen food.

'Why don't you have rulers?' Richard was saying. 'Because of the cuts?'

Amy ignored him.

'Well, hop in.'

'I can't. It's too high.'

Richard gauged the distance up to the cab with a critical eye.

'I'd have thought it would be a doddle for someone like you,' he said. 'Can't you vault in? Or do a back somersault up the hub cap?' He leaped back and landed, feet together, hands in the air, palms up, like a gymnast who has just completed a successful routine. He did not look at all like a gymnast in any case, and his donkey jacket made him appear even less like one. Amy thought that the neighbours might be watching and, embarrassed, glared at the kerb.

'I might tear something.'

'I did tell you to wear old clothes,' Richard said.

'These *are* old.'

'Then it won't matter if they get torn, will it? Look, I'll show you.'

He reached out for the handlegrip near the door hinge and sprang up, all in one movement via the hub of the wheel, like a cat going up a wall.

'Come on,' he said, peering down at her as he slid along the seat to his own side, 'or I'll go without you.'

Amy forgot the perilous ascent. This time she swung the bag up into the cab without worrying about where it landed and leaped after it.

'Told you it was easy,' Richard said. He was stowing her bag on the shelf that ran the width of the cab behind the seat. She guessed that she had hit him with it. 'Shut the door – hard.'

Amy reached out and pulled the door to with a clang. Now that the engine was going the whole cab was clanging, whirring, rumbling, entirely on the move even while the vehicle was stationary. The rear view mirror vibrated, the gear knob shuddered, the seat was trembling. Amy was astounded by the size of it. Her feet did not touch the floor and the seat was upholstered in uncomfortably shiny black plastic fabric. She groped crossly on either side.

'Where's the seat belts?'

'We don't have them.'

'But that's against the law.'

'Not in HGVs.'

'In whats?'

'Heavy Goods Vehicles.'

'What are they?'

'Lorries.' Richard spoke very slowly, like teachers at school did to the infants. 'This-is-a-lorry.'

'But it's dangerous.'

'Not if I'm driving it.'

'No – I mean, no seat belts.'

'Only if we hit another lorry – or a bus. Or a brick wall.'

'*That's* dangerous.'

'I've been driving for eighteen years,' Richard said, 'and I've never hit anything.'

'Has anything ever hit you?'

'Not head on.'

'From behind?'

'Yes – look, Amy, it would need a tank to hit us from behind before we felt anything.'

'Suppose we jack-knife.'

'You can only jack-knife an artic,' Richard said, patiently. He was adjusting a switch on the speedometer dial.

'Is that an alarm clock?'

'This is the tachograph. It records my speed, and the distance I've gone, and how long I've been driving.'

'Why?'

'In case I go too fast or stay on the road too long. It spies with its little eye.'

'What does it spy on?'

'Me.'

'Can it tell if I'm here?'

'No it can't!' Richard shouted, above the revving of the engine. 'It's not a bleeding Radar scanner!' And they were off.

Amy's first thought was, This is like flying, and she could not imagine why. They certainly did not feel airborne, the vehicle was definitely on a road, roaring and shivering, grinding over the tarmac, and they were nowhere near so high up as they would have been on the top deck of a bus. Then she realized that it was the view. The broad sloping windscreen began far above her head and ended below the level of her knees. There was no sensation of having anything between herself and the sky or the road. She turned her head to look at Richard and he seemed quite different; no bigger, he would never look big, but solid, in control, like a pilot, his hairy hands firm on the wide steering wheel. She had never noticed before that he had hair on his hands. Mr Smithies at school had hair right down to the beginnings of his fingernails, but his hair was dark and wiry and he was known as King Kong because of it. The hairs on Richard's hands were light and she could see them only because the early sun, shining between the houses, made each one gleam as if it had an electric current running through it. He slowed down at the end of Hurricane Crescent and turned into The Runway. A couple of hundred yards along The Runway they turned again, into the slip road, passed under the flyover and then they were on the A2. Every time they turned a corner Richard's box of maps slid from one end of the rear shelf to the other, hit Amy's bag and slid back again.

'Damn that,' Richard said. 'I usually keep it anchored. I forgot to put the Blutak back after I fetched it in yesterday. Can you fix it down?'

'I feel sick if I turn round in buses,' Amy said.

'This isn't a bus.'

'Can't I do it when we stop?'

'If you don't mind the row till we do.'

Amy was annoyed with herself. She had meant to take a last look at everything, as they passed it – the house, the end of the crescent, the shops, the pub – in case she never saw any of it again if they crashed messily on the motorway, or so that she could be properly homesick if they broke down on a desolate road Up North during a thunderstorm. She kept imagining a breakdown, and there was always a thunderstorm.

Instead, she had been so busy examining the flying sensation that she had scarcely noticed that they had left the estate until Richard put his foot down and she realized that they were on the A2. Home and the estate were already nothing more than roofs, shouldering over the swell of a low hill. The highest roof was on the sports hall of the secondary school, then that too had gone and all she could see of Gravesend was the shining smokestacks of the cement works on the river, and the long neck of a distant tower crane that, as she watched, slowly turned in her direction, as if giving her a last farewell look, and then swung back again.

Chapter Five

'But when are we going to stop?' Amy asked.

'Hungry?'

'No, but you were going to ring Mum.'

'Plenty of time for that.'

'Suppose she rings us?'

'She can't – no phone in this lorry. We're a bit old-fashioned.'

Amy could not tell whether he were being sarcastic or not.

'But if she rings home –'

'She'll think you're at school and I'm shopping. She won't be worried, if that's what you're worried about. *You* stop worrying. There's a place along here that I usually pull in at on this run. Not much further. I'll ring from there.'

Amy was not altogether looking forward to the first stop.

It would be at a transport café, she guessed, and she had wild ideas about what transport cafés were like: greasy vinyl floors, dirty formica tables awash with slops and floating swollen fag-ends, thick chipped mugs of fierce brown tea, oily platefuls of sausages and chips and baked beans, tomato sauce bottles with gory crusts round the necks, the dark air solid with cigarette smoke and made hideous by juke boxes and space invaders, while through the fume and gloom and the steam from the coffee machine, moved Neanderthal lorry drivers and sinister ladies with dyed blonde hair and nylon overalls. There would be enamel signs on the fascia and damp noisome toilets round the back. The transport café stood in a gritty car park where oil swilled in dingy rainbows over rain-filled puddles, and bare scrubby thorn bushes rattled dolefully in the wind. Discarded coke cans clanked in the overflowing waste bins and wallowed sluggishly in the flooded pot-holes, while white spectral scraps of paper cartwheeled lethargically over the tussocks of bleak winter grass in the dismal field beyond the hedge that stretched on and on to the treeless horizon.

'Out you get,' Richard said. Amy blinked, woke up and refocused on the road. It had gone. Richard had stopped the lorry in a layby and in front of them was not the rolling tarmac that she had last seen but a weeping willow tree, just coming into leaf, and hanging over a garden wall. On the far side of the road were some nice-looking semi-detached houses. Amy thought that someone might object to the smelly presence of the lorry in these surroundings.

'Why have we stopped here?'

'You'd like a drink, wouldn't you?' He flicked the switch on the tachograph. 'There's a phone in the café, too.'

Amy looked all round. 'Where's the café?'

Richard was already out of the cab. The door clouted itself shut and Amy found herself marooned until he came round and opened her door.

'Out you get,' he said again. He was so far below her, looking up.

'How?' said Amy.

'Jump. You're the gymnast.' There was no alternative unless she scrambled down backward as she had come up, over the hub. She jumped, and Richard caught her.

'Steady on. You don't have to do a double back somersault here to finish off with, you know.'

Amy thought that it was foolhardy of him to make jokes about gymnastics, under the circumstances.

'But where's the café?'

'Just back here. I did point it out, but you were dreaming.'

'I wasn't.' She had not been dreaming. She had been having a nightmare. 'I was counting catseyes.'

Richard turned into the porch of a red brick building beyond the far end of the layby. The porch, running the length of it, was also floored with red brick and there were brick pillars to support the tiled roof. It looked like a superior kind of health centre but a sign in the window, in front of the delicate white net curtains, said TEA, COFFEE, SOFT DRINKS AND LIGHT REFRESHMENTS SERVED ALL DAY.

'We can't go in here, can we?'

'Whyever not?' Richard said.

'But . . . the lorry . . .'

'We aren't taking the lorry in,' Richard said. 'It'll be quite safe in the layby.'

'But don't they mind?'

'Why should they? We're quite clean. We're going to pay for our coffee. We shan't put our feet on the table and strike matches on the wall. I'm not going to throw food about, are you?' He opened the door and Amy followed him in.

It was warm and quiet inside. Wooden tables and chairs stood on a green tiled floor. Music, very polite music, swelled gently from a loudspeaker on a shelf among house plants and trickled down through the trailing leaves. There was no formica, no space invaders, no crushed cigarette ends bloating in spilled tea. It was a lot nicer, in fact, than Sally's Pantry, up on the estate, where Mum sometimes took Amy and Helen for a drink on Saturdays, while they were shopping.

'Coffee?' Richard said.

'Yes, please.'

He went to the counter, which was not rigged with hissing coffee machines like a scaled-down oil refinery, and was kept by a respectable little woman who looked like Gran, and came back with two cups, in saucers. The crockery was made of white glass with a pattern round the rims, the same as in Sally's Pantry. There were biscuits, too.

Richard sat down and hung his donkey jacket tidily on the back of his chair.

'Does that tacky thing know we're in here?' Amy said.

'Tachograph. It knows we've stopped.'

'How?'

'I told it. I have to alter the mode switch if I'm taking a break or unloading. Then I have to put it back to "Driving Mode" when I start again.'

'Why?'

'So it knows whether I'm moving or not. We aren't allowed to drive for more than four hours without a break.'

'Suppose you can't find anywhere to stop?'

'That happens more often than you might think. The real limit's eight hours a day. You head for a lorry park in, say, Newbury, and find that the rules have been changed. Big sign up: NO LORRIES. Same with the transport cafés – they close down suddenly. You think you're coming to one and when you get there you find it isn't there any more.'

'What happens if you can't stop, then?'

'I'm breaking the law.'

'Even if you can't help it?'

'As soon as I go over the eight hours I'm breaking the law, and if I'm parked in the wrong place I'm breaking the law.'

'Can't you fiddle it?'

'The tachograph? No – that's why it's there. We call it the spy in the cab.'

'Why d'you have it, then?'

'It's the law again,' Richard said. 'For safety. A driver who stays on the road too long might fall asleep at the wheel. Think what a mess that might make – in a Scammell, for instance.'

Amy had no idea what a Scammell might be but she took his point. 'Oh, it saves lives.'

'You sound like a Government Health Warning,' Richard said. 'I dunno; the sort of people who used to break the law go on breaking it anyway.' He shrugged himself back into his donkey jacket. 'Fit?'

'Fit what?' Amy said, thinking he meant the jacket.

'Are you fit – fit to move?'

'Oh, yes.'

'Want the loo? It's over there, with the little lady on the door.'

'I wonder what they have in Scotland?' Amy said.

'Eh?'

'Well, you can only tell she's a lady by the skirt. I wonder what they do in Scotland, with kilts. Do the little men have skirts, too, on the gents? How can they tell which is which?'

'Strike a light,' Richard said, ungratefully. 'You made a joke.'

Steep walls rose on either side of the road.

'Are we going under ground?' Amy said. 'It's like the Dartford Tunnel.'

'Dartford Tunnel goes under the Thames. We went over it.'

'I *know*. But it looks like this.'

They came out into daylight again.

'It's part of the M4 extension into Wales.'

'Are we on the M4?'

'M40 – or we shall be in a little while. On your right, the Hoover factory. Coming shortly, Northolt.'

'I've just remembered,' Amy said, 'you didn't phone Mum.'

'Oh God, so I didn't,' Richard said.

'You didn't do it on purpose.'

'I know I didn't.'

'I mean,' Amy persisted, unforgivingly, 'you didn't do it by accident. You didn't *not* phone by accident.'

Amy, too intent on making her accusation, had forgotten to take into account what Richard would say when she had made it. He did not look at her because they were being overtaken by a tanker loaded with noxious chemicals.

61

'What do you take me for?' Richard said.

Amy mumbled and counted catseyes.

'I forgot. I'll ring from High Wycombe, I promise.'

They drove on in silence, or at least as near to silence as they could get in the thrumming cabin. It suddenly occurred to Amy that she was sitting on top of the engine. It was down there, directly underneath her.

'What happens if it blows up?'

'*What?*'

'Suppose the engine blows up?'

'Not very likely. What makes you think it might?'

'Well . . . if it did, we're right on top of it.'

'Not quite,' Richard said. 'Move a couple of inches to the left – all right, five centimetres – and you should be OK. I was driving a van once and I picked up a hitch hiker when one of the piston heads blew. It frightened the life out of him because the connecting rod broke and went on revolving. It just kept clouting the inside of the engine – you never heard such a row. Mind you, if the piston hadn't stopped where it did it would very likely have carried on up, straight through the hitch hiker and the Luton, before continuing skywards.'

Amy thought that Richard sounded rather too poetic, given the subject. 'What happened?'

'Nothing. But if it *hadn't* stopped where it did and he'd been sitting where you're sitting now . . .'

Amy shifted hurriedly.

'Whyn't you warn me?'

'You didn't ask. Anyway, it's not likely to happen again.'

'It might.'

'You could say that about anything. A USAF Hercules might come down on the box just as we pass the runway.'

'What runway?'

'I told you, Northolt. We're just coming to it.'

'Is it an airport?'

'An airfield. They still call it an aerodrome, I think. Over on the right.'

They were travelling downhill now, maintaining speed, sucking up the road beneath them. Amy, looking in the left-hand mirror that stuck out like a lug on the far side of the door, was surprised to find the road still there, spinning away behind the rear wheels.

'This place always bothers me,' Richard said.

'What does?'

'Northolt. Look at the lamp posts.'

'They're just lamp posts.'

'Yes, they are *now* – but keep looking. Notice anything?'

'Oh.' The lamp posts, on either side of the dual carriage-way, and in the central reservation, had suddenly become very much shorter, as if someone had been past with a very large mallet and driven them further into the ground.

'Why are they so much smaller?'

'You ain't seen nothing yet,' Richard said. 'Now look.'

'Why are they like that?' The shorter lamp standards had given place to very short lamp standards, so close to the ground that they looked like fencing posts.

Richard grinned. 'I wasn't joking when I said a Hercules might land on the roof. See those lights over the hedge? That's the end of the runway. The planes take off over the road.'

'What – as low as the street lamps?'

'Not quite,' Richard said, 'but low enough. That's what bothers me. Those lamps are lower than the top of the box.'

'You mean, a plane might hit us?' Amy found that while she was watching the stunted lamp posts slide by she had drawn her head right into her shoulders.

'Not this time – unless it's badly off course,' Richard said, cheerfully. 'We're clear of the runway now.'

The lamp posts were back to normal height. Amy unfolded herself. 'Does Mum know about that?'

'The lamp posts? Of course she does.'

'Doesn't she worry?'

'Not about them, in particular, but she worries. Of course she does.'

'Don't you mind?'

'*I* worry about *her*.'

'Why? She's at home.'

'Accidents can happen at home,' Richard said. 'I don't know till I get back of a Friday whether you three are all right, do I? I do plenty of worrying, never you mind.'

They came to a roundabout. The box of maps began its travels up and down the ledge again.

'You never fixed that down when we stopped,' Richard said.

'You never phoned Mum.'

'Yes . . . well . . . this is Uxbridge Hill. See that water at the bottom?'

'The river?'

'The Grand Union Canal – over we go. We're in Buckinghamshire now. That's the last of London.'

'*London?*'

'London Borough of Hillingdon.'

'But it was all fields.'

'Still London.'

64

Amy looked in the mirror again and watched the last of London vanish over the hill top behind them.

'Did I ever tell you,' Richard was saying, cruelly, 'about that time I brought down the high voltage cable in Wales . . .?'

Chapter Six

'That's High Wycombe,' Richard said.

'High? But it's all low down.'

'Only because we're up on the motorway – and we're coming off it any moment now. When we get down to *that* road, there, you'll see how high it is. And we're going to one of the highest bits.'

They left the M40 by a slip road, passed under the dual carriageway and Amy saw how high High Wycombe was. It was not so much built as *stacked* on the sides of a valley, rather like the estate at home, only the hills were steeper and the town went on and on, climbing higher and higher. Amy got the distinct impression that it was on the move, that it had simply frozen because she was looking at it, like Grandmother's Footsteps, and that if she glanced casually away the houses and flats would reach the horizon and sidle over the top, leaving the valley empty and green again.

Richard pulled off the road into a layby, and halted.

'Are we stopping again already?'

'Not for a break – I just want to check the street plan.'

'And phone.'

'Later – there's no phone here.' He riffled through the maps in the box that was currently at his end of the ledge. 'And while I do, get this thing stuck down.'

'Where should it be?'

'In the middle.'

Amy knelt on the seat and anchored the box to the shelf. Richard was muttering, 'First left, second left, first right and keep going. Second block after the service station.'

'They have phones at service stations. Where are we going?'

'Would you believe Halcyon Towers? On the Chiltern Hundreds Estate? I've noticed,' said Richard, putting the lorry in gear again, 'that the most hideous places have the prettiest names, especially if they're council estates. Something that looks like a broiler house stood on end gets called Glastonbury Court. I mean, look at that lot over there – dead ringer for Stalag Luft Three – know what it's called? Aspen Grove. You should see Blackbird Leys at Cowley – in fact you will. At least ours is named after something nasty.'

'Our what?' Amy stared out at the rows of brick houses and concrete flats.

'Our estate.'

'It's named after war planes,' Amy said. 'The Second World War – we did a project on it at school. There used to be an airfield at the top of the hill, where the school is.'

'And war isn't nasty?' said Richard.

'We won,' Amy said.

'Oh, that's all right, then.' Amy looked at him sharply, but he was peering ahead at street names. 'Here we are. Do you know what a halcyon is?'

'No.'

'A kingfisher. Must be crawling with kingfishers, this place.'

Halcyon Towers was not quite the ugliest block of flats she had ever seen, but it was clear that whoever had built it had thought that giving it a pretty name would be enough to improve the appearance. She counted the windows, upward. There were ten floors and for the first time she gave some thought to what they were towing behind them, in the box. It was full of furniture.

'How far up have you got to go?'

Richard switched off the engine at that moment, so she heard him groan faintly. 'Probably up to the top with a wardrobe. When I get there they'll be out, or they'll have decided they don't want it, or the thing'll fall to pieces on the way up.'

'It won't, will it?' Amy said. 'Furniture, I mean – it doesn't just fall to pieces.'

'You want to bet?' Richard said. 'You haven't seen the kind of furniture I deliver. I'm ashamed to be seen with it, especially when the legs drop off as I'm carrying it upstairs.'

'Is it cheap?'

'And nasty. Nastier than it need be. Don't imagine everyone has the kind of furniture your dad makes – made.'

Richard had never mentioned Dad before. Trust him to get the tense wrong.

'Are you stopping here or do you want to come up? You could carry the drawers.' He was looking at his clipboard of invoices. 'It's a dressing table.'

'You can't carry a dressing table all the way up there.'

'Our dressing tables are quite light – papery, you might say. And it's only the third floor, but the drawers are a nuisance. It would be a help if you'd carry them. They have this tendency to slide out and then they're in six bits when you pick them up. Embarrassing. Can you manage the drop? I should go down backwards if I were you.'

Amy had been about to tell him that she would stay in the cab, thank you very much, but he had already decanted himself. As she looked towards the side of the cab she saw him retreating towards the tail of the lorry in the off-side mirror. Because of the surface curve of the glass he seemed to dwindle very rapidly, as if someone had worked a shrinking spell on him. If he had not at that moment turned behind the end of the box he would have disappeared anyway, she felt, simply too small to be seen any more.

She hurriedly climbed out on her own side and dropped to the ground, expertly backwards, landing with bent knees as if coming out of a vault. By the time she reached the back of the lorry Richard had lowered the tailgate. He put one hand on it and sprang smoothly up, turning, as he stood upright, to grin over his shoulder at Amy.

'You're not the only vaulter in the family.' He stooped and threw up the great shutter at the end of the box and Amy saw inside for the first time. She had thought that it would be dark, like the interior of the removal van that she had once seen parked in the crescent, but the roof of the box was translucent and the contents were palely lit from above. These contents were wrapped in sacking and polythene sheets, labelled and closely packed together as if surging forward in a panic to get out. Right at the front was the dressing table for Halcyon Towers. Richard removed its polythene wrap and glared at it critically.

'It ought to hold together until we get it upstairs.' He pulled it out on to the tailgate. 'Look at it, Amy. Chipboard, hardboard and cardboard. It's stapled together.'

Amy had been thinking that it looked rather nice with its white paintwork, gold beading and sinuous legs, until Richard slid out the drawers and handed them down to her. Now she could see how it had been assembled. When Richard had mentioned staples she had imagined the tough steel hoops that fastened the chicken wire to the fronts of the rabbit hutches at school, but they were not that kind of staple at all. They were the kind that Mr Smithies used for holding papers together.

'Sometimes,' Richard said, 'these things fall apart when you get them out of the box.' He jumped down from the tailgate and lifted the dressing table on to his shoulder. 'There's an art to handling furniture – only I'm not sure this qualifies as furniture.' He set down the dressing table, closed the tailgate and lifted his burden again.

'Looks impressive, doesn't it?' he said, tossing the dressing table around with one hand. 'I reckon you could carry this.'

They started across the road. Halcyon Towers had lifts but although Richard pressed the button several times, and there was nothing to say that it was out of order, the lift failed to arrive.

'Up we go, then,' he said, turning to the staircase. 'Good thing we're not delivering to the tenth.' He went ahead of her with the dressing table. Seen from underneath it looked even flimsier and he was very dainty about going round corners. 'You have to be careful about not marking the paintwork – where there is any,' he explained. 'And anyway, something might drop off. Make sure those drawers still have handles on when we get to the top.'

There were three doors on the third-floor landing and different loud music was coming from behind each. Richard put down the dressing table and knocked on number 2.

'Shall I wait out here?' Amy said.

'No – come in with me. You're van-boy this trip; van-girl.'

Amy shifted her grip on the three drawers and tried to look efficient as the music behind the door of number 2 died down and the door itself opened to the sound of latches and bolts being drawn.

'Mrs Barclay?' Richard said.

The woman in the doorway looked at the dressing table. 'No,' she said. Her eyes wandered uneasily. 'That's not ours.'

'This is number 2, Third Floor, Halcyon Towers?'

'Ye-e-s.'

Fancy not knowing where you live, Amy thought.

'But you're not Mrs Barclay?'

'No. Er, no.'

And fancy not knowing who you *are* . . .

'And you didn't order a Furnuco Regency dressing table?'

'Oh no, we've only just moved in. Barclays must be the people who were here before. There aren't any Barclays here. Not on this landing.'

'Really?' Richard said. The woman was closing the door. 'You don't have a forwarding address?'

'No – I don't know where they went. I never met them . . .' The door shut.

Richard looked at Amy, seemed about to say something, then shook his head and nodded towards the stairway. He said nothing at all until they got back to the lorry and he was lowering the tailgate.

'Perhaps we got the wrong floor?' Amy said. 'Shouldn't we try . . .'

'That,' said Richard, 'was Mrs Barclay.'

'But she said she wasn't.' Amy put the drawers on the tailgate and Richard swung up the dressing table.

'I'll bet you anything you like she was. She's changed her mind, that's all, and she's afraid to say so. Or her old man's changed his mind and she's afraid of him.'

'Perhaps she looked out of the window and saw you chucking it about.'

'Don't cut yourself,' Richard said, sharply. 'More likely she didn't realize what she'd let herself in for until she saw it close to, after all,' he added. 'High Wycombe used to be the centre of the furniture industry. People round here probably know what a dressing table ought to look like.'

'But won't Furnuco's find out?'

'They may. It's nothing to do with me,' Richard said, manoeuvring the dressing table back into the box. 'I only deliver their rubbish and run – or try to deliver it. Speaking of which,' he said, tucking the polythene sheeting round the rejected dressing table, 'I hope this doesn't happen too often before tonight or there won't be any room in the box for us to sleep.'

'What shall we do?'

'Camp underneath it,' Richard said, leaping to the ground again. Amy could not tell if he were joking or not.

The next delivery was halfway up a hill on the other side of the valley, but it was at a house this time and the owner was not at home. Amy began to think seriously about the prospect of spending the night under the box; it did not look as if they were ever going to get rid of the furniture that filled it. But the third time that Richard stopped – outside a bungalow: the homes seemed to be getting lower and lower, Amy thought. Perhaps the next one would be underground – a woman answered the door and owned up at once to being Mrs Bainbridge who had ordered a Versailles-style wardrobe, a chest of drawers and two bedside tables. Amy took charge of the bedside tables and carried them in on her own.

'Helping your dad?' Mrs Bainbridge said, holding the door open and anxiously watching Richard to make sure that he did not mark the paint as he stowed the wardrobe in a back bedroom.

'He's not my dad,' Amy said at once, and then wished that she had not when she saw Richard's eyebrows rise in alarm as he disappeared into the bedroom.

'He's my stepfather,' she mumbled.

'Oh, that's nice,' said Mrs Bainbridge, but she did not look so approving now. 'Shouldn't you be at school?'

'Holiday,' Amy muttered. 'See, my gran rang up . . .'

'*Don't* go telling people I'm not your dad,' Richard said, when Mrs Bainbridge had finished signing the invoice and they were back in the cab. 'They'll think I've abducted you.'

'What's abducted?'

'Oh hell . . . kidnapped.'

'I said you were my *step*father,' Amy said, already wishing that she had said nothing at all.

'Why mention it?' Richard said. 'She didn't really want to know all that about Susan going to Colchester and Grandad being ill. She was just being friendly.'

'I didn't think,' Amy said.

73

'Well, think next time,' Richard said. He did not look very pleased.

'Where are we going next?' Amy asked, to change the subject.

'Stokenchurch. Avery Court. That sounds good, doesn't it? It's probably condemned. A bedhead,' said Richard, flicked his mode switch and started the engine again, and they moved off. A bedhead: Amy was sorry that it was not anything larger. The removal of a bedhead from the box would not make very much difference to the congestion inside. She imagined them going to sleep standing up, each in a wardrobe.

They did not return to the motorway but left High Wycombe by a country road that climbed steeply among hilly pastures.

'These are the Chilterns,' Richard said. 'Stokenchurch is right at the top.'

'They look like the downs.'

'Same sort of thing.'

'You still haven't phoned Mum.'

'I forgot – you didn't remind me,' Richard said, self-righteously. 'I'll pull in at the next phone box. Keep an eye open and tell me when you see one coming.'

There were houses now, on either side of the road.

'There's one,' Amy cried.

'One what?'

'A phone box. You were going to stop and ring Mum.'

'I can't stop here,' Richard said, 'we'd cause a tailback all the way to West Wycombe.'

You're afraid, Amy thought, squinting sidelong at him. You're afraid of what she'll say. She thought he deserved it but all the same she knew how he was feeling. Telling Mum about it was undoubtedly the worst part of doing something wrong. 'I won't be cross if you *own up*,' Mum always said when she caught Amy out, trying to conceal something, but she was always extremely cross even if you did own up. Amy dared not wonder how she could possibly be crosser. It hadn't struck her that things might be just the same for Richard.

'What do you think of that place?' Richard said, in a falsely bright tone. Now it was his turn to change the subject.

Amy looked where he was pointing. At a T junction stood a gaunt shuttered house with turrets and battlements.

'It's empty.'

'That's what I tell myself,' Richard said. 'That's what we're meant to believe, but I'm not so sure. Sometimes when I pass here at dusk I could swear I see chinks of light and dark figures moving about in the garden. Then I think maybe someone lives there who shouldn't.'

'Like who?'

'Who do *you* think?'

'Monsters.'

'What sort of monsters?'

'Scary ones. Dracula.'

'Not *Dracula*,' Richard protested. 'Who wants second-hand monsters? Invent your own.' But Amy could not think of any and the conversation died away. Richard turned right, opposite the monsters' house, and on to an estate, reaching back into the map box for his street plan.

'It may not be on here,' he said. 'By the look of it the mortar isn't dry yet.'

'How will you know where to go, then?' Amy said. 'Hey – there's a phone box over there – on that corner.'

'If it's a new estate the best people to ask are the police or the fire brigade. If *they* don't know they've got to find out.'

'Why?'

'Suppose someone rings 999 and says "My house is on fire," and then they can't find it.'

'They'd see the smoke.'

'All right. Suppose someone rings 999 and says there's a man being murdered next door. Don't tell me they'd hear the screams. They'd have to know where to find the house, wouldn't they? Ah, panic over; it's on here.'

'Aren't you going to ring Mum first?' Amy said.

'Afterwards. This place is in the next street.'

'The phone box is just over there.'

'I'll ring afterwards. Really.'

'Mmmmm,' Amy said.

Chapter Seven

It was lunchtime before Richard made his telephone call, a very late lunchtime, by Amy's standards. At school she was on first sitting, at twelve.

'What's the next stop?' she said, as they turned back on to the M40 at Stokenchurch, by the Post Office tower. Amy was accustomed to the Post Office tower at Meopham, a wiry structure of struts and girders. This was a concrete column on the very brink of the Chilterns, with a cluster of aerials and dishes at the summit.

'Oxford,' Richard said. 'Now, what's at Oxford?'

There he went, teaching again. 'Phone boxes,' said Amy.

'I wasn't thinking of phone boxes,' Richard said.

'Don't tell *me*,' said Amy, under her breath.

'BL,' Richard said. 'The biggest industrial estate in Europe.'

'BL?' Amy said. 'Where they have the strikes?'

'Where they make cars,' Richard said.

'What about the university?'

'You'll catch a glimpse in the distance, but we aren't going into the city centre. It looks better from the ring road anyway, come to think of it. We've got a delivery at Cowley, then we'll have lunch.'

'Are we having lunch near a phone box?'

Richard sighed loudly; loudly enough to be heard above the engine.

This delivery was a wardrobe and a sideboard. There was now a large bay opening up in the back of the box and Amy was beginning to imagine what bedtime would be like in among the pale shrouded furniture. They could each have a dressing table and a wardrobe, chest of drawers and a fancy bedhead. Amy liked the velvet ones, with buttons.

'Are we going to a transport café for lunch?'

'We may as well eat in the cab,' Richard said. 'After I made all those sandwiches. You did bring the sandwiches?' Amy turned to the shelf and fossicked in her bag to make sure.

'I thought turning round made you feel sick?'

'I'm getting used to it,' Amy said, hurriedly.

They drove on, round the ring road, until they came to a layby and Richard pulled in. Amy sat and looked at the windscreen, straight ahead, and said nothing.

'I'll go and ring now, shall I?' Richard said. 'If I can find a phone box.'

'We passed one a little way back,' Amy said, 'where those boys were fighting on the pavement.'

'I hope I've got enough change,' Richard said, opening his door.

'You can reverse the charges. Gran won't mind.'

'She will,' Richard said, incautiously, 'if it's me.'

When he had gone, Amy dug out their lunch. Richard had got up extra early to make the sandwiches and fill the vacuum flask with coffee. Amy unwrapped the sandwiches and examined them critically. They were not very tidy, rather like beds that had been made in a hurry by pulling up the bedspread carelessly over a tangle of sheets and blankets (just how Richard *would* make a bed, Amy thought) but the margarine was spread thickly and the meat was in succulent lumps instead of slices. He had done something strange to the cucumber, too. Amy had never seen a cucumber come out that shape before. Richard had folded the sandwiches loosely in cling film and they were beginning to sweat a little and part company. Amy reassembled them and laid them out on the seat on paper napkins, half each, but that made Richard's pile look rather small. After all, he was doing all the work and he needed feeding up. She transferred two of the sandwiches to his pile, inserted two or three extra pieces of meat from her own, and squeezed the bread down flat. Now the beds looked as if the pillows had got tucked in as well.

Far away, down the road, in the off-side mirror, an ant-sized figure was just stepping out of a telephone box that looked as tiny as a lantern on a Christmas tree, and starting back towards the lorry. She stood two mugs on the padded shelf below the windscreen and poured out coffee. The driver's door opened and Richard reappeared. He looked subdued.

'Was she cross?'

'Very.'

'Was she cross with me?'

'Of course she's not cross with you. But she's furious about Thursday.'

'The gymnastics?'

'She says we'll be letting the school down.'

Well, we will, Amy thought.

'I should have rung sooner, she said.'

'Yes.' She did not add, 'I tried to make you.'

'She said it was underhand not to let her know before.'

Amy was surprised that he was telling her this, as he must have known that she herself was thinking it. 'How's Grandad?' she asked.

'They're going to see him this afternoon.'

Amy pushed his sandwiches along the seat. 'Didn't she say how he is?'

'No.' Richard stared through the windscreen, evidently recalling what she *had* said. 'But he can't be doing too badly or your gran'd be there with him, wouldn't she?'

'Eat up,' said Amy, prodding the sandwiches. 'They're nice.'

'They're a mess,' Richard said gloomily. 'I used too much margarine. We'll eat in a café tonight.'

'Where will we be tonight?'

'Cheltenham.' He sat and chewed a sandwich. 'I shouldn't have, should I?'

'What?'

'Made you come with me.' They each had another sandwich. 'But you do want to see that mill, don't you?'

'Oh yes,' said Amy. 'Don't spill your coffee.'

The roads in Cheltenham were wide and there seemed to be a park around every corner, but Richard's café was in a narrow back street that looked more like home. The lady behind the counter knew Richard.

'That your daughter, Dick?' she said, taking the order for rock salmon and chips. Amy, sitting at a table by the window, looked round in surprise at hearing him called Dick. He did not bother to explain that she was really his stepdaughter and Amy could see that no one minded one way or the other.

After supper they strolled back to the lorry park.

'What do we do now?' Amy asked.

'Bed,' said Richard.

'But it's only half past eight.'

'We've got to build the bedroom yet, remember,' he said, 'and it's a long walk to the bathroom.'

Amy had forgotten about the bathroom. 'Where is it?'

'That public loo down by the park gates – it's only five minutes.'

'Won't it be locked?'

'Not yet, but we mustn't hang about.'

He pulled down the tailgate and leaped up, reaching out a hand to help Amy.

'You'd think they'd invent something to make it go up and down, wouldn't you?' Amy said. 'I mean, it would be easier with the furniture, wouldn't it, if you could press a button and the tailgate worked like a sort of lift.'

'They have,' Richard said. 'It's called a Ratcliffe lift.'

'Why don't we have one?'

'We have,' Richard said, 'only the one on this box is bust.'

'Don't you always have the same box?'

'No – only the same cab. That's not in very good nick either,' he added, irritably.

It was gloomy inside the box but not entirely dark because

of a street lamp that shone eerily through the translucent roof. There was now a room-sized area at one end of the box. Richard opened a little tin chest that lay in one corner, took out a torch and switched it on. 'Hold that,' he said to Amy, and the box heaved with seasick shadows as she took it.

Richard unrolled a length of rope and stretched it from one side of the box to the other, tying the ends to the framework. Then he took the dustsheets that had shrouded the furniture and slung them over the rope like a line of very dirty washing that sagged badly. He stooped to raise one of the sheets and pointed through the gap.

'That's your room,' he said. 'This one's mine. Take the torch through and I'll set up your bed. You can unpack the sleeping bags.'

Amy set the torch on the floor and unzipped the long canvas bag while watching Richard's enormous shadow spring and crouch among the silent wardrobes and chests of drawers and dressing tables at the front of the box.

'We'll do the hot water bottles when we get back,' he said, straightening up so that his shadow soared suddenly towards the roof. Amy ducked under the dustsheets and peered out into the dark evening.

'It's raining.'

'I know. I can hear it on the roof. Bath *and* shower. It's not raining much – come on.' Amy grabbed her sponge bag and followed him over the tailgate.

The light in the ladies had broken. Amy hovered in the dank tiled entrance and heard Richard's footsteps dying away in the gents next door before groping her way in. It was cold and there was no hot water. Amy was glad that they would be washing warmly in the box and wondered if the water that came from the tap was safe to clean teeth with. It tasted different from the water at home.

Home: radiators, steam, soft towels that Mum had ironed and hung in the airing cupboard. The water in the pipes gulped and moaned, a cistern belched and slow footfalls went by in the road. Amy stuffed everything back into the sponge bag and rushed outside. A policeman was passing.

'What are you up to, then, young lady?' he said, neatly fielding her as she hurtled out and almost into the path of a car that was turning the corner.

'It's dark in there,' Amy wailed. 'The light's gone.'

'On your own, are you?'

'My – my – Richard – he's in the gents,' she said, wishing that Richard would come out now, this minute, and he did.

'Anything wrong?' Richard said.

'She nearly ran under a car,' said the policeman. 'Frightened of the dark.'

'Not frightened,' Amy said, quickly, 'but I couldn't *see* anything.'

They parted company with the policeman at the corner. Amy found that she was holding Richard's hand. She let go. 'Don't they talk funny here?' Amy said.

'That's only Gloucestershire,' said Richard. 'They think we talk funny, too. First time I came here someone took me for an Australian.'

'We don't talk funny.'

'We do, you know,' Richard said. 'We sound funny everywhere but in the South East. We'd sound even funnier in Wales.'

'Are we going to Wales?'

'Not this trip, but I'd like to take you there sometime. It's my favourite route.'

'Are there mills in Wales?'

'Mines. I've picked up a bit of Welsh. It helps.'

'Welsh? Is that what they talk?'

'Some of them. Why not? They speak French in France.'

'But Wales is part of England.'

'If we ever go there you'd better not say things like that,' Richard warned her.

'But isn't it?'

'It's part of Great Britain; so are we.'

The lorry looked almost cosy when they returned to it and climbed in out of the rainy darkness. Amy listened to the drumming on the roof as Richard pulled up the tailgate and shut them in for the night. He switched on the torch and from the tin chest in the corner took a little camping stove with a blue butane canister attached. There was a kettle in the chest as well. He lit the stove, filled the kettle from a plastic container and set it to heat.

'You get into bed when you've washed,' he said to Amy, 'and I'll bring your bottle through when it's ready. Do you want some cocoa?'

'Cocoa?'

'Well, drinking chocolate. Better not have too much, though; it's a long way to the loo, remember.'

Amy crept under the dustsheets to her bedroom and washed in the little plastic bowl that Richard had given her. Then she pushed it back, under the dustsheets to his side, and changed into her night clothes while he clattered about on the far side of the curtain. Every now and again his shadow lurched into view. She looked into the bag for Elizabeth Bear, but there was no sign of her. Amy remembered that Elizabeth was one of the things that she had been putting in and taking out last night, while sulking. She must

84

have been left on the settee and would still be there when they came home on Friday, looking more martyred and resigned than ever. Her eyes had been lost when Amy was little and Mum had embroidered some new ones with wool, but she had absentmindedly sewn them on the wrong way round, with the whites in the middle, so that Elizabeth seemed always to be rolling up her eyes to heaven in weary despair. Amy felt weary despair too. She had never wanted Elizabeth so badly.

'You decent?' Richard called, after a bit. Amy slid down into the sleeping bag's clammy tube as he ducked between the dustsheets with her hot water bottle in one hand and a mug in the other. Amy poked the hot water bottle down toward her feet and took the mug.

'I'll probably read for a bit,' Richard said. 'The light won't bother you, will it?'

'No.'

'If you get chilly, just put some more dustsheets on. Good night.'

He went back to his own room but after a moment his voice came across the screen. 'I've got a friend of yours here. Shall I send her over?'

'A friend?'

'Stand by. Here she comes,' and Elizabeth came spinning over the dustsheets, loose legs in autogyro. She fell on to the bed. Amy grabbed her and curled up in the sleeping bag with her chin drawn to her knees and the hot water bottle in the cave of her stomach.

'She must have fallen out when you got your sponge bag,' Richard said. 'You should let her out sometimes, in the cab. She might enjoy the view.'

Amy cuddled Elizabeth as she had not done for a long

85

while. Richard was not meant to know about Elizabeth. Mum thought it was time she went in the dustbin, being too old and scabby for Helen to inherit, but Richard seemed to regard her as respectable company. On the other side of the dustsheets his newspaper rattled and the rain tattooed on the roof. Amy lay awake, sure that she would never sleep, and fell asleep thinking it.

She was woken in the morning by a fearful slamming on the roof and sat up with a squawk, unable to remember where she was.

'What was that?'

'Eh?' Richard, in his own room, was not much worried, by the sound of it.

'It sounded like someone running along the roof.'

She thought he would laugh at her but he said, 'It was – a seagull.'

'But it sounded huge!'

'Seagulls have big feet. Go back to sleep, we've another hour yet.'

She heard him grunting his own way back to sleep immediately, but she herself was fully awake, her heart whirring from the shock of the seagull's take-off. She turned on her back and looked up at the early morning light that seeped through the roof in a dirty yellow fog. There was another thump, softer this time, and a small bird landed. She could see its dark shape moving about and heard faint clicks as it pecked. What would it sound like, she wondered, if a duck should pancake on the roof, or a goose? A swan, with its great slapping black webs, would probably come straight through.

She watched her breath rising from the murky dark where

she lay to the murky light above her. Overnight it had become terribly cold in the box. Her feet were turning icy and the hot water bottle was a dank lump under her knees, like something that had crawled into the sleeping bag and died in the night. She lay looking at the heap of dustsheets by the screen, debating whether or not she dared to crawl out into the deadly chill to pull one over her. And the floor looked dirty; not the kind of dirt that a quick run-round with a broom would shift, or even an industrial vacuum cleaner, but *filth*, thick sandy furry *filth* that would stain and stick to hands and feet and become *grime*, and turn to *muck* if it got wet. It had a permanent, undisturbed look, like the kind of dirt that you found at the foot of walls in garages and around gateposts after rain.

Mum would have a fit if she knew where Amy was now, under a dustsheet in a sleeping bag on a camp bed in a filthy old Luton in a lorry park in a back street in Cheltenham. Amy realized, little by little, that Mum's reluctance to let her travel with Richard had nothing to do with heavy traffic and freezing fog, missing school and the gymnastics – or very little: it was the dirt. It was the dirt.

'Where are we now?' Amy asked. Rain was sluicing the windscreen so hard that she could no more see what was going on the other side of it than she could through the reed glass of the front door at home. If reed glass were to dissolve it would look like this.

'Birmingham,' Richard said.

'But you said that ages ago.'

'Birmingham goes on for ages. You just be glad you can't see it.'

'Where are we stopping?'

87

'Birmingham.'

Amy skulked in her seat with her jacket drawn up round her ears. It was warm enough in the cab but the rain all round it made her feel sure that she was cold, and she was still clammy from her night in the box, rising in the dim cold, walking to the bathroom through the early morning drizzle, washing in chill Cotswold water. The water tasted funny, Richard said, because it ran through rock. He had pointed out how clear it was as they had crossed a river bridge. 'But just because it's clear doesn't mean it's clean,' he had told her. 'Don't go drinking it.'

'Out of taps?'

'Out of the river.'

Amy could imagine what Mum would say to that.

They had made two deliveries before breakfast, eaten at a transport café on the way out of town. Richard had read the paper over his plate of eggs, fried bread and tomatoes.

'I always check the firm's share prices first thing,' he explained. 'Make sure I've got a job to go back to. Eat up your sausages, Amy. You're not in training now.'

Amy thought wretchedly about the gymnastics then, for about thirty seconds, but all she could recall now were the sausages and bacon and thick coffee, hours and hours ago. She thought she knew now what it meant to be chilled to the bone.

Richard was scowling through the windscreen.

'This looks like it.'

He halted the lorry and immediately the glass cleared as the rain began to fall on it instead of hitting it head on.

'Double yellow lines,' Amy said.

'Can't help that. This is a big order.' He shifted the mode switch. 'I'm not humping it halfway along the High Street

88

'— anyway, the double yellow lines are to stop cars getting in the way of people like us.'

'Like what?'

'Lorries delivering to shops.'

'Furniture to a shop?' Amy said.

'It's a furniture shop,' said Richard.

Amy stared down at the oily puddles on the pavement, the bits of paper pasted to the concrete slabs like postage stamps, the wet floating fag-ends. In fact the pavement was very similar to the table top in her imaginary transport café. The transport café that they had had breakfast in had been shabby, but not dirty; cleaner than the box at any rate.

Mum wouldn't have wanted to eat there, though, Amy thought. She said, 'Do you need any help?' and hoped that he would say no.

Richard was apologetic. 'Sorry — but I do. There's a lot of carrying and there'll only be women to do it.'

'What's wrong with women?' Amy snapped.

'Nothing, but they can't shift so much at a time. Any extra help —'

'How d'you know it'll only be women?'

'It's a low-paid job,' Richard said. 'Don't you end up in a shop.' He reached behind him to the shelf and took up the clipboard.

'I want to be a dancer.'

'Better than being a gymnast,' Richard said, riffling through his papers. 'You'll be an old lady at twenty. This'll be the lot, then.'

'Lot of what?'

'Last delivery. After this we go to the depot, dump the rejects and the ones that fell apart, and load up again for the North.'

'The depot!' Amy said. 'Back to Gravesend?'

'No, this one's in Wolverhampton,' Richard said. 'Come on, take a deep breath and jump. You can only drown once.'

Amy took a deep breath, opened the door and jumped; and landed in Birmingham.

Chapter Eight

Wolverhampton was, if anything, even wetter than Birmingham had been. Amy looked doubtfully out of the window.

'In there? All by myself?'

'It's a café, not an opium den. Come on, Amy.'

Amy froze to the seat. 'I can't.'

'You can't come to the depot.' Richard's jaw was stiffening as if his temper might burst out dangerously if he opened his teeth. 'We've been into all that. You knew before we left –'

'That was a *different* depot.'

'It's the same *firm*. Look, just get out, will you?' Richard said. 'I won't be above an hour, at most. We're on double yellow lines.'

'We were on double yellow lines outside that shop and you said it didn't matter.'

'I was delivering, then.'

'Well, you're delivering now.'

'You don't count. Look, I'm nearly on a corner and I'm blocking an exit; now, Amy, *please*, get out.'

'But it's a transport café.'

'You've been in enough transport cafés by now.'

'But that was with you.'

Richard leaned across and opened the nearside door. 'Out!'

He loomed so threateningly beside her that Amy almost rolled out of her seat to avoid him and smacked down, flat-footed, on the wet pavement. Richard tossed her bag down and slammed the door, calling, 'See you in an hour', then, 'Don't stand there in the rain like a dying duck in a thunderstorm.'

Amy however did not move until the lorry had reached the end of the street and turned left. It was a horrible street, especially in the rain. On one side were concrete flats and scrawled walls covered in slogans for Wolves. She would not have been surprised to see wolves, at that, slinking from alleyways with slavering jaws and red eyes; or werewolves. On her own side was a row of small old terraced houses, each with one window and one door downstairs and one window upstairs. Water gushed and plopped and trickled from leaky gutters.

The corner house had had both its frontages rebuilt into plate-glass windows and its doorway, which bit off the angle of the corner, was screened by a green and cream venetian blind. A sign, stuck on the glass, said OPEN but the windows were so steamed up that Amy could not see what was going on inside.

It was a fool place to put a transport café anyway, Amy

thought, in a back street scarcely wider than a lorry, with double yellow lines on both sides.

She turned reluctantly toward the step up to the doorway and was about to venture in, out of the rain, when the door opened and a huge lorry driver came out. Amy blenched: it was the lorry driver of her nightmares, a hugely fat man in a boiler suit built for two, boots that were surfaced like concrete rendering so long was it since they had been polished, and a donkey jacket with a vinyl reinforcement panel across the shoulders. His arms were short – they seemed barely to reach his waist – and his head was tiny, sprung with greasy coils of hair and lidded with an old cheese-cutter cap. He swelled out of the doorway as if someone were inflating him through a nozzle from behind and at high speed. When he saw Amy, almost underfoot, he rose upon the horny toes of his boots as if about to break into a heavy and horrid ballet dance. Behind him, as the door swung in the wind, Amy saw steamy shadows and a coffee machine, cigarette smoke and sauce bottles. It was the transport café of her nightmares.

The lorry driver beamed down benevolently over his paunch like the sun peeping over a dense fog bank, and said something. Amy, clutching her bag, was too terrified to listen and in any case his accent was so wide and flat and astonishing that she could not make out a word. Instead she gaped and nodded violently.

It seemed that he had been asking her if she wanted to come in, for he stood gallantly aside and held the door open with a fat friendly arm.

'Thank you,' Amy said, now unable to remain outside in hygienic safety, and dodged under the arm as if expecting a weighted blade to descend on her neck from the angle of his armpit. The door closed at her back and triggered an electric bell that sneered shrilly at her: *Yaaaaaaaaaaarrrrrrrrrr*.

Amy looked round the café. Even on a spring morning with the birds singing outside it couldn't look better than it did now. Even at midnight in smog it could hardly look worse. It was the whole downstairs of the little corner house with a kitchen at the back behind the counter, and it was crowded with tables and chairs. All but a few of the chairs were swamped with large damp lorry drivers; the air smelled of smoke and frying, onions and damp lorry drivers. A radio was playing loudly. Amy was amazed to hear that it was playing a tune that their own radio played at home in Gravesend. No one took any notice when she came in and after a moment she realized that no one would even look at her if she behaved normally. They would only turn and stare if she stayed where she was by the doorway, staring at them and clinging to her bag as if it were a lifebelt and she adrift in a raging sea.

The floor was covered in streaky red and white lino, like the tray of bacon bits in International, but grimily puddled with rain from wet boots, and from the door to the counter someone had laid a causeway of cardboard made from old grocery boxes, squashed flat. SURF it said on one of the boxes. Amy thought of surf boards and great curling green waves, and drowning, and trod very carefully on the boxes after that in case one of them skidded on the lino and carried her with it, careering across the floor.

Behind the counter was a girl with dyed blonde hair and a nylon blue smock. She seemed surprised when she saw Amy approaching and leaned across the counter. Amy, sensing that she was indeed out of place, simply because she felt out of place and therefore looked it, wished herself outside again.

'D'you want something, love?'

The girl was even harder to understand than the lorry driver had been. She sounded as if she were speaking against the pressure of a powerful spring in the back of her throat, but Amy could guess what she was saying by the way she said it.

'Is it all right if I wait for my stepfather?'

In spite of what Richard had said about being taken for an Australian in Cheltenham it had not struck Amy that the girl might find *her* accent funny, but she could see that she did. But she smiled, at any rate.

'Of course it's all right. Do you want a cup of tea?'

'Yes, please,' Amy said, cursing herself. Of course, she should have asked for a cup of tea, that was what the place was for, only she was convinced that the tea would be the same colour as the puddles on the floor and taste as though it had been wrung from a rain-soaked donkey jacket. However, it was just tea, and the cup seemed clean. Amy took it and looked for somewhere to sit. There were no entirely empty tables but over by the window was one with only two drivers sitting at it. The table top was not too clean, Amy noted, and the red plastic seat of the chair had a sooty, grainy look, but after her ratty wash this morning in the Cheltenham ladies she felt too grubby to care.

'Is it all right if I sit here?' she asked.

One of the drivers looked up. He was quite young, like Richard, and quite tidy. Amy felt safer.

'Help yourself,' he said. She could tell by his voice that he came from the South and was pleased with herself for noticing.

'On your own?' he asked, as she sat down and balanced the bag on her lap. Amy hesitated. Mum had warned her often enough about speaking to strange men, and so had PC Mizen who came up to the school to tell them about road safety, especially strange men who spoke to you first and offered you sweets.

This one just offered her the sugar, which was normal because it was at his end of the table. Anyway, with so many people around and the nice girl behind the counter, he would not be able to do very much.

'I'm waiting for my – my – for Richard, for my stepfather,' Amy said, accepting the sugar bowl. It had a brown crust round the rim. 'He's just taking the lorry back to the depot to pick up another box.'

'Who's he with?' the other driver asked. He looked quite ordinary too, and wore an anorak instead of a donkey jacket.

'Me,' Amy said.

They both laughed.

'No, I mean, who's he drive for?'

'Furnuco,' said Amy.

'Haven't they gone bust yet?' said the first driver, but the other said, 'Oh, that lot out on the A42. But you're not from round here, are you?'

'Gravesend,' Amy said.

'Nah!' The man seemed astounded. 'Hear that, Derek?'

'What?'

'She's from Gravesend.'

'What part?' Derek asked.

'Britton's Field Estate. Up near the A2.'

She was glad she knew what road it was. She had

just thought of it as the main road until Richard came along.

'Small world,' said Derek. 'I used to live up Chalk Way. Other side of the Rochester Road.'

'That's nice,' Amy said, and then remembered that she was talking to strange men and began drinking her tea, very hard.

'What's your name?' asked Derek's friend.

Amy gave him a beady look to prove that she knew what he was up to. 'Amy Calver.'

Derek's friend looked at Derek.

'Don't know any Calvers, do we?'

'Only bloke I know from Furnuco's is Dick Ermins.'

'That's him!' Amy cried. 'My . . . my stepfather.'

But they were still strange men, even if they did know Richard. She went back to her tea.

After a bit Derek and the friend got up to go and said goodbye, asking her to give their regards to Richard.

Amy said goodbye too and watched them leave with growing suspicion. Why were they in such a hurry to go? Perhaps they didn't really know Richard at all and wanted to leave before he came back and denounced them as impostors – no, that wouldn't do. They had mentioned him first. But why had they not waited to see him? Amy moved up to the empty chair where Derek had sat and rubbed a bald patch in the furry steam on the window pane. By leaning hard on the cold glass she could see right along the street. She sat there, gazing into the wan Wolverhampton daylight, and wished that Richard would come.

When he did come it was at a run, head down and with his collar turned up, through the hissing rain. The road was awash and the rain was hitting it like gravel from a chute.

The café was half empty now and he had no trouble spotting her when he dived in through the doorway. *Yaaaaaaaaaarrrrrrrrr*, said the bell, but not spitefully this time.

'Good news,' he said.

'Where've you *been*?' Amy cried. 'You've been ages.'

'There was a lot to do at the depot. Then I stopped off to phone – want the good news?'

'Phone who?'

'Susan. That's the good news. Your grandad's going to be all right, they think. Too soon to be certain but she says they're very hopeful.'

'Is Gran all right?'

'Everyone's all right. Helen . . . Susan . . .'

'Is she still cross?'

'Helen?'

'Mum.'

Richard's smile grew a little dim. 'Yes, but not *so* cross, because of your grandad. Don't worry, she'll probably have left off being cross at all by the time we get back. Anyway, she's not cross with you.'

'No.' Amy felt that in fact this would make no difference. If Mum were cross with Richard, Amy would feel it just as much. When Richard was unhappy you *knew* about it, just from being with him, even when he said nothing. If Mum were still angry with him by the weekend he would certainly be unhappy.

'More tea?'

'Could I have orange, this time?'

'Tea's more warming. It's filthy out and getting colder.'

'Yes, but this tea's sticky.'

'As you like. Do you want a bun?'

'Can I have one of those curled-up ones with currants?'

'Chelsea bun. Look, Amy, when I rang, I didn't tell Susan how bad the weather is.'

'But she'll be watching the forecasts. She always does when you're away.'

'Does she? I should think she'd have something better to worry about at the moment, but she won't know how bad it is here – not unless there's floods and we get on the news. Anyway, don't say anything.'

'But I can't.'

'Well, I told her you'd ring tonight, from Stoke. If you want to, that is.'

'Of course I do.'

'Well, don't say anything that'll make her fret, eh? There's nothing to fret about, but you know what she's like – better than I do, I expect.'

She nodded and he went to the counter for their order. Amy wondered what she would say to Mum, in Stoke, wherever that was. She had been saving up a list of grievances, the cold, the wet, the *dirt*, the ladies' toilet at Cheltenham, but, of course, this was not what Mum would want to hear.

Then she realized that perhaps it would be just what Mum wanted to hear, so that when they came back she and Richard could have a proper row, with yelling, instead of everyone clamming up and tiptoeing about shutting doors carefully. Amy did not think that Mum would have left off being cross when they got home. Mum would want a row and she could not have a proper row if Amy came bouncing in saying that she'd enjoyed herself.

Richard came back with tea, orange juice and the buns on a plate.

'You having one too?' Amy asked.

'Not if you want them both.'

'Oh no. I didn't know you liked buns.'

'I like unwinding them,' Richard said, and he did messy things with his Chelsea bun that Mum would never have allowed, uncoiling it into a long doughy strip and picking out the currants. Amy did likewise.

'I'm getting you into bad habits,' Richard said. 'You'd better not do that when we get home.'

Amy grinned and said nothing because she had been thinking the same thing.

Richard wiped his hands, drank his tea and pulled a moist map out of his pocket.

'Do you want to see where we're going? Come over here then, it'll be easier.'

Amy moved round to the chair beside him and Richard opened the map. 'Can you see where we are?'

Amy thought fast, wanting to get it right first time. The last stop had been Birmingham. Birmingham, she knew, was the second largest grey patch on the map, smaller only than London, so they must be . . .

'Here!' she said, seeing the word WOLVERHAMPTON and pointing.

'Right, well done, now –' he traced a blue motorway with his finger, 'as soon as they've finished loading the box –'

'I thought we were having a new box?'

'We are, but guess what? The Ratcliffe lift has jammed on this one too.'

Amy was disappointed. She had been longing to see the Ratcliffe lift in action.

'Anyway, as soon as it's mended – sorry, loaded – we'll be

off up *here* and stop overnight in Stoke-on-Trent. See? Tomorrow we go on to Manchester.'

Manchester was the third largest grey patch.

'Where's Oldham, then?'

'Here, to the North.'

'Aren't we Up North, yet?'

'No, this is the West Midlands,' Richard said.

'Will we see the mill tomorrow?'

'Oh, definitely. Even if the route doesn't go near it we'll make a special trip.'

'What about the tachograph?'

'The tacho doesn't say where we've been, only how long it takes to get there. We'll probably leave the lorry for the evening and go and look on foot, or take a train. The railway passes quite close.'

'It's real, then.'

'What's real?'

'My mill.'

'Of course it's real,' Richard said. 'You didn't think I was having you on?'

'Oh no.' Amy paused. She had not imagined that he was lying to her, she simply had not believed him. It was not quite the same thing.

'It's there, all right,' Richard said. 'Mona, Dawn, Amy and Coral.'

'Is there a Helen, too?'

'No,' he said, 'just Amy.'

Chapter Nine

'I don't believe it,' Richard said. He gazed through the windscreen. Then he said, 'Yes, I do, though. It's always happening.'

Amy stared too. It had only recently stopped raining and in the wet and shiny evening light the lorry park looked rosy, serene almost; only it was no longer a lorry park. Someone had fixed a bar across the entrance at a height that would only just admit a minibus, with a notice in the middle that said, rather unnecessarily, NO LORRIES.

'Why've they done that?' Amy asked.

'Perhaps they were afraid we would break up the surface,' Richard said, sourly.

The surface looked as if it had been shelled. The sunset lay in oily pink puddles, some of them three metres across.

'Could we break it up any more? Where can we go?' She imagined them driving round Stoke-on-Trent all night with nowhere to park and the tachograph silently recording their every illegal move.

'Oh, there'll be somewhere else, I think,' Richard said. 'This isn't *so* bad. The real nuisance is when it happens on the road. Up comes the Law and says, "You can't park here," and I say, "But my tachograph says I mustn't drive any further," and the Law says, "But you *mustn't* park here," and I say, "But I mustn't drive either," and the Law says, "That's your problem." '

'What happens then?'

'Like the man says, it's my problem. I remember heading for a café once and when I got there I found they'd closed it and turned it into a garden centre; gnomes and plastic storks everywhere.'

'They could have ponds here,' Amy said, looking at the flooded pot-holes, 'with water lilies and plastic storks.'

'I'm not all that fond of plastic storks,' Richard said. 'Oh well, off we go again.'

Amy had once seen a picture of Stoke-on-Trent in an old history book at school, which had been left on the table outside Mr Smithies' office, ready for throwing away. It had looked like the nastiest place in the world with rows of identical cramped houses and factories and dirty churches and strange smoking buildings that resembled brick milk bottles. Thinking back she realized that this photograph had been the picture of what she had thought Up North must be like, but even Wolverhampton in the rain had not been quite so dreadful – parts of Gravesend were worse than Wolverhampton in the rain, she was forced to admit – and Stoke-on-Trent was not dreadful at all. If you had to make a list of towns in order of preference, she thought, Stoke-on-Trent would be somewhere up near the top, as high as

Gravesend at least, perhaps even higher. There were hills round Gravesend, she lived at the foot of one, but they were all outside the town. Stoke seemed to be built on hills. There were wide views and valleys, but nowhere could she see a brick milk bottle. She was sorry about that. She had been looking forward to the brick milk bottles.

It took Richard another twenty minutes to find a place to park.

'Haven't you been here before?' Amy asked in some desperation.

'Not for a while,' Richard said. 'They seem to have moved all the roads since last time.'

Amy could not be sure that he was joking. Quite a lot of Stoke-on-Trent seemed to have been moved since that photograph was taken.

'Hah!' Richard said. 'I see a man.'

'Where?'

'Coming down the street. He's on your side, Amy. Open the window and ask him where Bidulph Street is.'

'Me?' Amy said.

'Yes. Quick.'

She gaped at him hopelessly. How could she possibly yell down from the cab at a complete stranger who would, very likely, be unable to understand her? She wouldn't be able to understand him, either, and he did not look friendly.

'Open it.'

'I can't.'

'Why, is it stuck – here, let me –'

'I *can't* ask him . . .'

'Why not? Oh, come on, girl.' He was getting angry again. The man on the pavement drew level and passed by below them.

'You're off your head,' Richard said, crossly, and leaped down from his own side to catch up with the man, leaving the engine running.

Amy, abandoned with the droning motor – what if the brakes should fail? She stared at the brake warning light – hunched herself into a small heap on the seat. In the mirror she could see Richard talking to the man from Stoke-on-Trent. They were both pointing and nodding. The man looked quite affable now. He was laughing. Amy felt more foolish than ever.

But how could I *know*? she muttered, telling herself that there was no way she could have known in advance that the man was all right. How could *I* know?

Richard was coming back to the cab, growing huge and threatening, in spite of looking so tiny, in the mirror. He climbed in.

'You're daft,' he said, briefly.

'I'm sorry,' Amy said.

The lorry moved forward.

'What were you afraid of?'

'I thought I wouldn't be able to understand him.'

'Oh, come off it. You've understood everybody else so far.'

Amy mumbled.

'*What?*'

'I don't like talking to strange men.'

'He *wasn't* a strange man.'

'Yes he was. I didn't know him.'

'How can you get through life without talking to people you don't know?' Richard shouted. 'Aren't you ever going to speak to anyone except me and Sue and Helen and Old Mother Varley – or do I count as a strange man too?'

'Don't be silly.'

'Who's being silly? How did you manage when you started school?'

'That was different.'

'No it wasn't.'

'Yes it was. I knew people.'

'You can't always have known them. You weren't *born* knowing them.'

'Anyway, they weren't strange men.'

'What's all this with the strange men?' Richard demanded.

'Mum says I mustn't talk to strange men – and PC Mizen.'

'You mustn't talk to PC Mizen?'

'No! He says so too.'

'But what did you think he could *do*?'

'PC Mizen?'

'No – that bloke back there. I was here. Did you think he'd come swarming up the side of the cab and drag you out of the window?'

Amy glared at him out of the tail of her eye. He was not angry any more, she could tell; his voice had changed. He was laughing. Suddenly he pointed. 'Look – there – it's the last one in Stoke, I believe.'

Amy looked quickly where he pointed. It was her brick milk bottle.

'Oh.'

'D'you know what it is?'

'No, but I wanted to see one. It looks like a milk bottle.'

'It's a bottle kiln. They called them pot banks.'

'A what?'

'A pot bank. A kiln for firing pottery.'

'That's not a kiln,' Amy said, watching the pot bank disappear in the mirror.

'It is.'

'It's not like our kiln at school,' Amy said.

'It's a real kiln. That's what they used to use, once.'

'Oh – in the photograph,' Amy cried suddenly, 'with smoke coming out of the top.'

'You've seen a photo of one?'

'Yes, only there were lots of bottle things then. It was ever so old. I suppose that's why it's called firing.'

'What is?'

'When you bake pots, they must have used to light real fires with smoke, in those milk bottles.' She thought of the craft room at school, and it did not measure up very well. 'Ours is just square, like an oven.'

After they had parked the lorry they went on what Richard called a recce, as he did not know the area. 'Bathroom first,' he said, 'then dining room.' He meant a convenient public convenience and a café. They found the first a couple of streets away from the lorry park and the second ten minutes' walk from that.

'Shall we have Chinese food?' Richard said.

Amy had acquired a taste for Chinese food. 'Isn't it expensive?'

'Not so very – anyway, it's been a hard day. Let's break out a bit.'

'Aren't we too dirty?'

'What, to eat in a Chinese restaurant?'

'Any restaurant.'

'I suppose we are, a bit. Tell you what,' Richard said, 'let's go back to the bathroom – has it got hot water?'

'It has on my side.'

'Right, we'll have a really good wash, put on some decent clothes and be respectable. Would you like that?'

'Yes, please,' Amy said. 'Look, there's a phone box. Can I – ?'

'Yes, they should be home by now. I'll wait here. Reverse the charges – do you know how?'

'I haven't done it before.'

'Hah! Who told me *I* ought to reverse them?'

'Well, I *know* about it – I've just never done it. I don't know what to say.'

'Just ring the operator and say you want to make a transferred-charge call to Colchester and give her the number.'

'It might be a man.'

'He's going to get you over the phone, is he?'

'I didn't mean that. I just thought it might not be a her.'

'Go on, then.'

'I might get it wrong.'

'How can you?' He saw her face. 'All right, I'll do it.'

When they had squeezed into the telephone kiosk Amy began to wish that she had made the effort to do it herself. Richard, she could tell, was beginning to think that she was an idiot. And she did not know what to say to Mum with Richard only half an inch away, but once he heard the ringing tone he handed her the receiver and stepped outside.

'Don't be too long, it'll cost your gran a fortune.'

Mum's tiny distant voice came over the line from Colchester.

'I have a call for you from Stoke-on-Trent. Will you accept the charge?' the operator butted in before Amy could say anything.

'Yes,' Mum said.

'Go ahead, caller,' said the operator, but Amy could think of nothing to say and said nothing.

'Hullo? *Hullo*,' Mum was saying, at the other end. 'Who is it? Richard?'

'Mum?' Amy said.

'Amy?'

'How are you?'

'I'm all right, how are *you*?'

'I'm all right. How's Grandad?'

'He's much better. Listen, Amy –'

'Yes?'

'I'm sorry about all this.'

'All what?'

'Well, you missing the gymnastics and that. I know you didn't want to go with Richard. He shouldn't have –'

'It's all right,' Amy said. 'It's interesting. I've seen a pot bank.'

'A what bank?'

'Pot, a pot bank. Pot's pottery. And tomorrow I'm going to see a cotton mill with my name on it.'

'I don't know *what* you're talking about,' Mum snapped. 'I told Richard he oughtn't to have –'

'It's all right. I'm having a nice time. Thank you,' Amy said.

'*A nice time?*'

'Yes. We're going to eat Chinese tonight. It's nice, Mum. It *is*.'

Mum made a very strange noise, far away in Colchester. It sounded like 'Goodbye'.

Amy said goodbye too and hung up. She felt very strange. It had not been like talking to Mum at all, more like talking to Richard. She looked out of the kiosk and saw him walking tactfully up and down a little distance away.

Only, of course, talking to Richard was no longer like that.

Stoke-on-Trent seemed even more cosy and familiar in retrospect when they got among the hills next day. Amy had never imagined that hills could be so steep in England; they made High Wycombe look like an ant heap.

'Where are we?'

'Cheshire,' Richard said.

'Where the cheese comes from?'

'I don't know. I suppose it did once. It's probably made in Taiwan these days – hush a minute.'

'What – ?'

'Shsh!'

Amy shut up and listened. She did not need to be told what to listen for. Something bad was happening down below in the engine, something chronic, that thumped. She remembered Richard's tale of the broken con-rod.

'Is it the piston head?'

'No.' The thumping stopped.

'Is it all right, now? What did you do?'

'Changed gear.' Richard was frowning. Apparently even the fact that the noise had stopped was not good news. It started again. 'Third gear's breaking up.'

'What'll happen?'

'It'll break up. If they'd only service these damn things regularly . . .'

'But what'll happen when it does?'

'We'll stop. Sharpish. Now, don't start flapping. We'll be

stopping anyway in a few minutes, for a delivery. I'll phone through to the yard and ask what they want me to do.'

'What *can* you do?'

'What I'd like to do is get it fixed locally, but if I know our mob they'll tell me to try and get back to Wolverhampton – which I shan't – shan't try. But we ought to make it to Stockport.'

'But the gearbox. Will it blow up?'

'Blow up? You've got blowing up on the brain. When did you ever see a vehicle blow up?'

'On telly.'

'This is a gearbox, not a car bomb,' Richard said.

Amy laughed but she could see that he was worried and that any more daft questions would not help the situation one little bit, so she sat quietly and only wondered, instead of asking, what would happen when the third gear cog did break up.

When they reached the delivery point she had never been so glad to hear the engine shut off, and it was not until then that she realized that she had been clinging to the back of the seat and sitting with her eyes squeezed tight, for the last ten minutes as the lorry dragged its way upward. Now, when she opened them, she saw what she had been missing on the way up. It was a sight to make the blood rush to the feet, a valley that seemed to drop away from beneath their very wheels, down and down, until it was combed level and swept upward into a great green crest on the horizon.

'What's that mountain?'

Amy jumped down from the cab and stood staring, on the hill top.

'Chest of drawers and two bedside tables,' Richard

murmured, walking round to join her. 'That's Kinder Scout. I don't know whether it's a mountain or a hill.'

'What's the difference?'

'Now you're asking. Mountains come to a point, don't they?' Richard said, on his way to the back of the box. 'Actually, I guess it's a peak. That's the Peak District over there.'

'Where are *we*?'

'This is Disley. Stockport next, then Oldham.'

'What about the gearbox?'

'Whatever happens we're going to Stockport. Then we'll get the gears seen to and it'll be Oldham after that, even if we are a bit behind schedule. We'll get to Oldham eventually, don't you worry.'

'And my mill?'

'And your mill.'

'Did you bring the camera?'

'Yes, but I haven't put a film in it yet. We'll get one when we've done this drop – and we'd better look out for presents for Sue and Helen.' He was on the tailgate, calling, 'Got any ideas?'

Amy thought for a moment while he handed down the bedside tables.

'I know what she wants, but it's more like for birthday or Christmas.'

'Never mind; what is it?'

'A steam iron.'

'Oh, *Amy*!' He shouted it.

'What's the matter?'

'That's not a present. Can't you think of something useless?'

'She doesn't want any more plants,' Amy said, warningly.

'When I've got the greenhouse together we can put all the plants in that,' Richard said. He looked wistful.

'You could get her a plastic plant. Some of them look ever so real, and you can wash them.'

'And a plastic gnome to go with it, I suppose. I'll think about it.'

'And she needs some more oven gloves.'

'I could buy her a new dustbin,' Richard said, ferociously, and lifted down the chest of drawers. It stood solidly on the tarmac for a moment and then, quite slowly, the back fell off.

'One of those days,' said Richard, and Amy remembered the gearbox.

Chapter Ten

Amy kept telling herself, 'It could be worse. We could have hit something,' but she knew perfectly well that she had no idea what it would have been like to hit something. The fact that they had broken down was as bad as it needed to be.

Rejoining the main road out of Disley they had found themselves at the end of a tailback that edged very slowly toward Stockport.

'That's all we need,' Richard shouted above the horrid clangour from the gearbox. 'Some nutter taking his JCB for a stroll, I suppose – or a funeral. Did you hear the one about the construction worker who won the pools? He bought a JCB GT. Oh God, here we go again, change up, change down, keep moooooooving. Hang on to the seat, Amy. I'm going to get out of this as soon as I see a layby.'

He had seen the layby just in time, and only just in time, for as he signalled to turn left the third gear broke up entirely with a terrifying racket as the fragments fell in among the other cogs, the wheels of the lorry locked and they skidded into the layby. The lorry stopped dead, Amy clutching the back of the seat, Richard the steering wheel.

'That's something you *don't* tell Susan about,' Richard said, 'well, not for a few weeks, anyway.' After that they sat in silence for several minutes, thinking about what might have happened.

'We could have hit something,' Amy said to herself again. Her hands were leaving damp prints on the black plastic upholstery.

'You're sure you're all right?' Richard said.

'Yes. I wasn't hurt, or anything.'

'Shaken up?'

'Only a bit. We shan't get to Rawtenstall tonight, shall we?'

'Shouldn't think so. Still, it's not the end of the world if someone in Bacup doesn't get their horrible Furnuco wardrobe tonight. It's probably fallen in half, anyway. They'd do much better to hang their clothes on the carpet. What a good thing we don't make carpets.'

'I wasn't thinking of that,' Amy said.

'No? Oh, good. I wouldn't want you getting too interested in that rubbish in the back.'

'We shan't be able to see the mill, shall we?'

'Oh God.' Richard looked guilt stricken. 'I'd forgotten about that. I was going to hitch into Stockport –'

'You aren't going to leave me here?'

'Of course I'm not going to leave you here. We'll go together. Then I'll get someone out to look at this, but I don't know how long it will take and there may not be much time tomorrow. Look, do you mind very much?'

'No,' Amy said, gazing out of the window. The whole reason for the journey had disappeared, collapsed like the chest of drawers, disintegrated like the gearbox. They didn't have much luck with gearboxes, she thought, recalling the car at home. Then she began to remember that tomorrow was the day of the gymnastics competition and here she was, the team reserve, stuck on a hill in North Cheshire.

'You do, don't you?'

'No, I don't, really.' They were being polite again. They had not bothered to be polite for days; it had been almost like travelling with a friend, and now it was all gone.

'Hang about,' Richard said, after a brief bleak pause, 'I've got an idea. You don't want to stick around in Stockport, do you?'

'No,' Amy said unguardedly, being unable to see the drift of his thoughts.

'And you want to see the mill?'

'Of *course* I do.'

'So you do mind, really.'

'I did *want* to see it,' Amy said.

'Well, you can. I'll take you into Stockport with me and put you on a train.'

'To *Oldham?*'

'Oh yes. You can get to Oldham by train. I told you. It's an easy journey, all you have to do is change in Manchester.'

'Change trains?'

'Yes, well.' He looked away. 'Change stations.'

'*Stations?*'

'Yes, but it's so easy. I don't know why I didn't think of it sooner. All you have to do is get a train at Stockport and Manchester's the next stop.' Not noticing, or deliberately ignoring, her expression, he went on, very rapidly, 'This chap told me that all the Inter-City services have to stop in Stockport because the viaduct doesn't belong to British Rail, it belongs to Stockport Council and they said –'

'I can't go to Manchester by myself!'

'– and they said, "If you don't make your trains stop at our station we won't let you use our viaduct." '

Amy thought of the great grey blob that was Manchester, only slightly smaller than Birmingham – and look at Birmingham.

'*Richard*, I can't. I don't want to. Mum would be furious.'

'Why?' Richard said.

'She won't even let me go into Gravesend on my own. I might get lost. There might be a strike or something, or an accident. I don't know the *way*. I've never *been* to Manchester before.'

'You can't get lost in Manchester,' Richard said. 'There's this bus –'

'I don't *want* to.'

'Yes you do. You want to see your mill. Listen, no *listen*. Amy, it's so easy. You get on at Stockport and you get off at Manchester Piccadilly.'

'Piccadilly's in London; with Eros and all those signs –'

'This Piccadilly's in Manchester. You go outside the station, through the main entrance, and the bus stop's right outside. There's a bus every ten minutes. You just get on, pay your fare and get off at the other end.'

'How shall I know where the other end is?'

'It's Victoria station.'

'But that's –'

'Manchester's got one too. You can't miss it; you know what a railway station looks like. Then you go in, get on the

117

Rochdale train and look out of the left-hand window until you see Amy. I can't quite remember where it is but it's before Rochdale, I know. Then you get out at Rochdale and catch the next train back to Victoria and do the whole thing in reverse. I'll meet you at Stockport.'

'I can't,' Amy said.

'Why not?'

'I can't. I might get lost.'

'You can't get lost on a train.'

'And someone might – might, someone . . .'

'A strange man?' said Richard.

'Well, they *might*.'

'They might up on Britton's Field Estate,' Richard said. 'Manchester's only a place, you know. It's full of people like us, and Susan and your gran, people shopping and going home from work and schoolkids. It's broad daylight.'

'Mum says things can happen in broad daylight.'

'If you let them. If you get worried the best thing you can do is go and find a woman with kids or an old lady with shopping. They're usually pretty safe.'

'It's not funny,' Amy growled.

'I know it's not, love,' Richard said. 'Horrible things can happen, but they probably won't. You're a sensible girl. Anyway, you can't spend the rest of your life not going anywhere unless you're with Susan.'

'It's different when you're grown up.'

'I know – but you've got to *start* growing up, or it won't be. You'll always be afraid.'

'Mum won't half go on.'

'She won't go on at *you*.'

'I'd rather not.'

'I think you should,' Richard said, 'because you may not

118

see the mill, otherwise. You wanted to tell everyone at school, remember?'

'Well, I can still tell them it's there, can't I?'

'But you won't have the photograph.'

'I don't mind.'

'You will when you get back.'

'I can wait till next time.'

'I shouldn't think there'll be a next time, to be honest,' Richard said.

'You can take one for me, next time *you're* here.'

Richard turned to her and put his hands on her shoulders. 'Amy, tell me the truth; *why* don't you want to go?'

'It isn't safe.'

'You'll be safe if you do exactly what I told you. If anything goes wrong, people will help. They're just the same here as they are at home – nicer if anything.'

He sounded so kind that Amy began to feel tears coming. Almost she wanted to go because he so much wanted her to.

'You'll be so pleased when you've done it.'

'I'm frightened.'

'So am I.'

'Why're you frightened?'

'Well, not frightened – but worried. Still, at least I'll know where you've gone. If you'd gone off without telling me I'd be frightened all right. You were late home one Saturday once – it was getting dark. You'd stopped off with some friends at the swing park, but I didn't know that. I was just coming out to look for you – and it was only half past four that time.'

'When was that? I don't remember.'

'Last November – just after we got married. Sue had gone into town, shopping.'

'You didn't say anything.' Amy remembered suddenly. 'You were cross.'

'Only because I was afraid – same as Sue would be, but this time I'll know where you are, every inch of the way. I trust you – can't you trust yourself?'

Richard's method of hitching a lift was simple. He stood by the roadside and held out a tachograph disc, and the first lorry that passed them stopped.

'Sort of code,' Richard said, as they ran toward the waiting lorry, 'but don't let me catch *you* doing it.'

'What?'

'Hitching. That really would be stupid.'

The lorry that had stopped was loaded with fifty-gallon drums. At first Amy could think of nothing but what might happen if they came loose on one of the hills, or if this lorry lost its third gear cog, but after a bit she forgot about what was behind them and began to think about what lay ahead.

It did not take long to drive into Stockport and far too soon, in her opinion, they were back on the pavement and walking up the road to the station. The approach was up a long ramp. Amy plodded beside Richard who had fetched out a fat paperback book from the map box, before they abandoned the lorry. It was the British Rail National Timetable and its supplement.

'Bought it at the station after that panic on Saturday,' Richard said. 'I'm not getting caught like that again.'

'Why a supplement?' Amy asked, thinking of Sunday papers.

'Some of the schedules change during the year,' Richard said, and Amy panicked again in case he had made a mistake about exactly which ones had changed. The time-tables were in small, terrifying print.

'Even if I have made a mistake there are plenty more trains,' Richard said easily. 'Here comes yours. Oh, you're in luck. A flying banana.'

Round the bend in the track came an Inter-City 125, yellow locomotive at either end. Amy could see why it was called a flying banana. 'Remember what you've got to do?'

'Yes,' Amy said. No sound came out.

'Got the camera?'

She nodded.

'Got your money?'

'Yes.'

'See you at six, back here. Don't worry if you miss the five forty-eight, there's plenty more. I'll wait.'

The 125 drew alongside with a savage roar from the front locomotive. 'Be quick – they only stop for a few moments. Actually,' he added, opening the nearest door, 'you're not really meant to get on this one –'

Amy squeaked in alarm.

'– only no one's looking. Go *on*.' He pushed her gently up the steps. 'They're only meant to set down here. Take care.' As he closed the door he pulled down the window and as the train began to move again he reached in and kissed her.

'Have a good time – and don't lean out.'

Instead Amy leaned back against the bulkhead so that she could see him walking along the platform and waving his timetable. When he, and the station, were out of sight, she went to find a seat.

The 125 was not like the trains at home. The carriages were made up of single compartments divided only into smoking and non-smoking. Amy was disconcerted when the door at the end of the compartment opened by itself with a thud, to let her through, and then closed again. She sat down in the nearest empty seat and looked out of the window. This was Up North as she had always imagined it; factories, houses, power stations, chimneys. She waited to feel afraid and for a few minutes nothing happened, then she recalled what was waiting for her in Manchester and she felt properly afraid. She recognized the feeling at once and knew that it would go on and on, and get worse, but before she could really settle down to concentrate on it the train, which had scarcely gathered speed out of Stockport, began to slow down again. A platform slid alongside the window. The compartment grew dark under a high roof of iron and glass, like in the main line termini in London, and the train stopped. They were in Manchester.

All round her people were collecting coats and luggage. Amy had no luggage, only the camera in her pocket. She waited until everyone else had left the train and then got out herself. Richard had put her in a carriage near the middle and she was a long way down the queue for the barrier. There was time to stop and worry. This was where things could begin to go wrong.

There would be no buses. She would lose her money. A pickpocket would steal Richard's camera. No one would be able to understand what she said. She would not be able to understand what anyone said, like the lorry driver who had given them the lift to Stockport. She had been sure that he must be foreign but Richard said no, from Newcastle. All his words had seemed to have a hinge in the middle of them.

She had reached the barrier without noticing it.

'Ticket, love?' the inspector said. Amy did as Richard had

told her. She waved it and said 'Return,' and it worked. Now for the bus. Now for no bus.

There was no bus, but there was a bus stop and a queue. Amy tacked on to the end of it and after a bit an orange bus drew up. She got on, paid her fare and sat down. That was all. It was just the same as buses at home, except for the colour. It did not need looking at so she looked out of the window instead, at Manchester. It was just buildings and people, like Stoke-on-Trent, like Cheltenham, like Gravesend; only bigger. There seemed to be more room but that was all. Even the people looked the same, they only sounded different like . . . like . . .

They sounded like 'Coronation Street'. Amy began to feel safer.

As Richard had forecast, Victoria could not be taken for anything but a railway station and it had its name up on the wall. Amy, and everyone who was still on the bus, got off and went inside. She began to feel frightened again. There were so many platforms, so many trains, and not very long before hers pulled out, according to the British Rail National Timetable. She would have to ask someone, but Manchester Victoria reminded her of London Victoria, where people snapped if you spoke to them as if they were afraid that you might take advantage of their good nature otherwise. But there was no help for it. She went up to the nearest man in uniform.

'Yes, love?'

'Where's the Rochdale train? Please?'

She thought he would demand to know why she was travelling alone, and did her mother know she was out, but he just smiled and pointed to a board which said, very plainly, MILES PLATTING, DEAN LANE, FAILSWORTH, HOLLINWOOD, OLDHAM WERNETH, OLDHAM MUMPS, ROY-

TON, SHAW, NEW HEY, MILN ROW, ROCHDALE, so she said 'Thank you,' and he said 'My pleasure,' and as there was no barrier here, she got on the train.

This one was hardly a train at all, just three coaches joined together. It was old and smelly and Mum would have put newspaper on the seat when she saw the dust that whirled like smoke in the golden afternoon sunshine. Amy sat down with a thump and it rose in dense clouds. There were still five minutes to go. She rehearsed the names, Mona, Dawn, Amy, Coral. After seeing what the local stations were called, it no longer seemed strange to her that cotton mills should have names, not after Miles Platting and Oldham Mumps.

The train had reached Hollinwood before the conductor came along, clipping tickets. Amy handed him hers, he clipped it and gave it back, by which time they were clear of the station. She realized that she was on the wrong side of the train and moved across to look out of the window. The train gathered speed. Amy thought of Richard, in Stockport. She was getting further and further away from him.

Perhaps he wouldn't be there when she got back. Perhaps it was like Hansel and Gretel, where the wicked stepmother sends the children into the forest to lose them.

Richard as a wicked stepfather was such a silly idea that she grinned, the first grin for days, it seemed. A woman sitting opposite saw the grin and smiled too. Amy made her own smile last a little longer, to be friendly, and turned back to look out of the window. She was just in time for there, sliding out of sight, was a great brick building with a tower at one end and on the tower, in tall white letters, was the name Mona. It was the first mill.

Amy took the camera out of her pocket and pointed it out

of the window so that it would get used to the light. She hoped that the train would be moving very slowly when they reached Amy. If it went any faster than it was going now all she would get would be a blur.

There was another – Dawn. They looked like enormous brick churches, except for the windows.

The train had only just pulled out of Oldham Werneth when it began to slow down again. Amy, eaten up now with impatience, willed it to move on, but she felt the brakes dragging at the wheels and as the train came to a halt she looked up and there, just opposite the window, was the third mill: Amy.

The window was filthy. Amy sprang up, ran to the door of the carriage and tried to pull down the window in that but it was stiff with age and grime. She tugged at it furiously. Any moment now the train, which must have stopped at a signal, would move on again and Amy the mill would be lost to view.

Seeing her struggling, the woman who had smiled got up and hurried to help. 'What's up, love? Are you going to be sick?'

'No.' Amy could not help laughing. 'I want to get a picture of the mill and the window's too dirty.'

The woman tried too, but the window was firmly stuck. Amy had not thought of anything like this going wrong, something annoying; only of catastrophe.

'Give us a hand,' the woman cried, and a young man who had been sitting on the far side of the carriage ran to help. Between them they forced the window open. Amy raised the camera, lined up the viewfinder and took the picture, just in time, for as she pressed the shutter release the train gave an awful jerk and began to move again.

The woman closed the window.

'Bit of a draught, else,' she said. They all went back to their seats.

'What was all that for, then?' the young man asked. 'A keepsake?'

Amy put the camera away. 'It's got my name on it.'

'Your name's Amy too?'

'Yes, after my gran. Why's the mill called Amy?'

'I never thought,' the young man said. 'I expect it was named after the wife or the daughter of the owner.' He turned to the woman. 'Takes a foreigner to catch you out over your home town, doesn't it?'

Foreigner. Still, they were all understanding each other.

'There used to be nearly two hundred,' the woman said, 'once upon a time. Did you come specially to see yours?'

'Yes. My dad's a lorry driver and he brought me all the way Up North to see that mill, only the lorry broke down and I had to come on my own, by train, or I wouldn't have seen it.'

'Where've you come from?' the woman asked.

'Gravesend.'

'Where's that?' said the young man.

Amy was shocked. 'Kent.'

'You've got to go all the way back to Kent on your own?'

'Oh no. Only to Stockport. My dad's meeting me at Stockport.'

'Well,' said the young man, 'if you get off at the next stop you can get a train back to Victoria.'

'No, thank you,' Amy said. 'I'll go on to Rochdale.'

'This'll be quicker,' the woman said. She began to gather up her shopping. 'I get out here.'

'No, my dad said Rochdale. He wrote down all the times for me.'

The woman smiled again as the train drew into Oldham Mumps. 'Best to do what your dad says.'

She got out and Amy watched her walk down the platform and then the train moved on again, only five stops now to Rochdale, where she would get out and wait for the connection back to Manchester Victoria, where she would catch the bus for Piccadilly, where she would board the train for Stockport, where Richard would be waiting.

The train was slowing down for Royton. The young man stood up, ready to get out, and paused beside Amy.

'This your first time up north, then?'

'Yes.'

The train stopped and he jumped down to the platform. Then he poked his head back inside the compartment.

'And what do you think of it?'

'It's all right,' Amy said. 'It's nice. It's just another place.'